Pr̲

BODIES OF CONSEQUENCE

'This is another impressive, thought-provoking and articulate work by Chong. His mastery of language and ability to engage the reader's imagination and spiritual sensors, through the power of a story, is again engrossing. This is a wonderful story, littered with reality and connections to the divine (the hereafter) and our Spirit. It is a provocative work as to why we do what we do. Why we make the decisions we make. Why we spend sometimes little time on the consequences of what we said or did or simply believe.'

Mario Calanna – Calanna Pharmacy Group
Author of *Design a Good Life: From Farm to Farmacia to Whole Health*

'Rarely, so rarely a book appears that at once captivates, engrosses and enthrals whilst evoking the empathetic emotions that can ordinarily only be experienced whilst watching a movie. This book engages the senses by drawing graphic pictures of Life and the Afterlife, weaving a masterful story of humanity.'

Universal Storyteller

'A riveting portrayal of life in the hereafter as a consequence of life and the choices we make. *Bodies of Consequence* is a once in a lifetime book not to be missed.'

Dr E. M. Martin
Author of *Journey Beyond the Self*

BOOKS BY STEPHEN CHONG M.Ed.

The Book of Testaments: A Practical Guide for Spiritual Realisation

The Music of the Soul: A Pathway to a Rich and Fulfilling Life

Letters Across Time: A journey of enlightenment

The Power and the Possible: A Teenager's Traverse of the World

FEATURE FILM SCREENPLAYS

Bodies of Consequence

A Meaningful Life

The Power and the Possible

Mean Paradise

The Pivot Point

Stephen Chong M.Ed.

BODIES OF
CONSEQUENCE

INGRAMSPARK

AUSTRALIA

Stephen Chong/IngramSpark
www.stephenchong.com.au

Publisher's note: This is a work of fiction. Names, characters, places, and incidents are a product of the author's imagination. Locales and public names are sometimes used for atmospheric purposes. Any resemblance to actual people, living or dead, or to businesses, companies, events, institutions, or locales is completely coincidental.

Text editing and book design by Dr Juliette Lachemeier@ The Erudite Pen: www.theeruditepen.com

Cover designed by Christian Hildenbrand

Bodies of Consequence/ Stephen Chong –1st ed.
ISBN 978-0-6484579-0-9

Acknowledgements

If it were not for the love of my family, neither I nor this book would be here. Thank God for their love or I'd be in heaven, somewhere!

CONTENTS

Prologue...1
CHAPTER 1 5
CHAPTER 2 11
CHAPTER 3 19
CHAPTER 4 27
CHAPTER 5 35
CHAPTER 6 45
CHAPTER 7 53
CHAPTER 8 63
CHAPTER 9 73
CHAPTER 10 85
CHAPTER 11 93
CHAPTER 12 101
CHAPTER 13 111
CHAPTER 14 119
CHAPTER 15 131
CHAPTER 16 147
CHAPTER 17 157
CHAPTER 18 169
CHAPTER 19 181
CHAPTER 20 191
CHAPTER 21 199
CHAPTER 22 213
CHAPTER 23 219
CHAPTER 24 227

CHAPTER 25 237
CHAPTER 26 249
CHAPTER 27 259
EPILOGUE 265
Author's Note 269

Prologue

Matthew J. Cooper, Age 20
France, 1944

I heard the soft jangle of the dog-tags around my neck as I took a calming breath to still my mind. I knew the inscription by rote: Cooper, Matthew. J. Service Number: 346890, Blood Type: O-positive: Religion: Nil. I wondered vaguely whether the tags would be fit for purpose if I didn't survive today's orders.

I felt the sharp pang of a twig that prodded my ribcage for attention. It pulled my mind back to the here and now. After all, this is what I was trained for. Ever since I was a boy, I'd held a rifle in my hands. The harshness of life in outback Australia had taught me many things. The main one being that I learned to 'harden-the-f**k-up', so I didn't mind the slight physical discomforts – they were a part of the job. But the soft lichen and dried leaves of the canopy floor of the European autumn even provided a remembrance of comforts long forgotten – a bed, a bath, a warm meal. They were a blessing compared to the muddy filth and cold of the long war-time winter months.

I took a deep breath. It stilled my mind and aided the waiting. Forever waiting. In any case, that was what the job required. I was good at it. Even as a child I would sit for hours on end – just watching – animals and birds mainly. Kangaroos, wallabies and brush turkeys were a specialty in my outback. The watching made me feel powerful. Silence – no abrupt movements – everything in slow motion. I moved my right hand ever so slowly towards the adjustor on the telescopic lens. Range approximately 750 metres, an easy distance for one of my skills.

I sniffed the breeze. It held a slight hint of cordite, probably from the heart of the affray a few kilometres to the west. I could even feel the thud of the heavy artillery through the wavelengths in the ground on which I lay, slightly elevated as I was from the enemy line. I focused my attention through the aperture. I knew a target would appear – they always did. So I waited as seconds passed to minutes to hours. I didn't really notice the passing of time. It always proved a great time to delve into the many compartments of my rather full memory banks. If there was one thing this war had done, it had filled up a shit-load of room in my memory.

There was a room I always loved to visit. It was like returning home to the warmth of a blazing hearth and the sound of my mother in the kitchen cooking dinner. Mind you, there were other rooms that I feared to enter. I heard the horrible screaming of a child as I passed one door. The heat coming from behind that entrance to hades felt like a dragon's inferno breathing ravenously from inside. I certainly wasn't going in there! My pace quickened as I moved speedily through my memories to a more pleasurable chamber.

It was her sweet scent that flooded my senses even before I turned the handle. Even so, my hand shook as I pushed the door in my mind ajar. Her sweet caress and the touch of delicate fingers on trembling skin – it was real, I could feel it. I wondered vaguely whether she would still be waiting for me when/if I ever returned from this hell. Would she still feel the same? Unbidden, I felt my manhood rise in semblance to forgotten pleasures. That just wouldn't do! I was working. I had a job to do, so slammed the door firmly shut and kept walking.

I didn't know what lay behind one of the other doorways – I couldn't bring myself to look – but I could hear the sound. It was like a hundred voices crying in unison, a sound both sweet and terrifying at the same time. It made my pulse race and beads of sweat appear on my brow. Not much good for my present situation. The fear of these memories made my hand tremble again, and that just would not do. I shook my head slightly to bring my mind back to focus on the war in front of me.

In an instant, a target appeared. I knew it would. They always did. My steady index finger tightened then squeezed. The recoil of the rifle caused a familiar jolt to my shoulder blade. I didn't mind; I'd felt it a thousand times before, like a jolt back to practised reality. I watched as the blood spread evenly across the enemy's chest, just to his left of centre. I didn't know whether to smile or cringe. I was just doing my job, after all.

I exhaled as I mused, *How many was that now?* I wasn't sure, fifty, a hundred? Maybe more. I'd stopped counting months ago. I wasn't keeping a scorecard or anything. I was just doing what I was good at.

I didn't get up straight away, that just wouldn't do. The enemy would have a fix on my position. I could hear the bark of their dogs and could sense the telescopic apertures scanning the perimeter for any trace of my presence – so I waited until the afternoon sun decided to shun further comfort to those under its waning warmth. *No point getting dead for something you know not to do*, I thought.

CHAPTER 1

Matthew J. Cooper, Age 66
Outback NSW, Australia, 1990

The open window and curtains of the lounge allowed a gentle breeze to cool the room as the television bleated away in the corner about the current news of some disaster or other. The noise somehow gave me comfort. I heard my daughter, Mary, shuffling about in the kitchen making dinner for the family. She was a good woman. I was proud of the kin I had raised.

Sitting comfortably in the recliner, I smoothed my grey, thinning hair and watched absently as my nine-year-old grandson Michael played happily on the floor. He had plastic toy soldiers aligned in adversary and pushed over those he considered dead enemy combatants.

'Hey, Grandpa, is it true that you fought in the war?'

The surprise question raised me from my reveries.

'Yes, my boy, I was,' I replied.

'Did you kill anybody?'

The question made my hand tremble slightly on the arm-rest. I looked at the limb as if it was an alien part of my body. *I wonder why it is shaking now*, I thought? It had never shaken before under pressure.

'Yes, I killed a lot of people. That was my job,' I replied.

The boy pushed over another enemy combatant and smiled, 'Pow! Gotcha ... Right in the heart. You're dead, bad man.'

'Wow, Grandpa, I bet that felt good, didn't it. To kill the bad men, I mean!'

It didn't really serve to delve too far back into my war memories but I figured the lad needed the benefit of my wisdom if he was to grow into the prospects of a fine young man.

'I guess, my boy, it's not about what you feel. It's about doing what's right.'

The boy's brow creased in complexity before a smile once again lit his innocent face.

'I get it, Grandpa,' he said. 'When you go to war, it's about killing as many of the bad men as you can. Kill or be killed.'

I figured that was about as much wisdom I was capable of and tried to turn the conversation to something else – unfortunately, the inquisitive young mind was locked onto purpose.

'But Grandpa, how many did you kill?'

The question opened a door in my mind, and I heard both the sweet and terrifying sound of a hundred voices crying in unison.

'Look, my boy,' I said with more ire than I should have. 'It's not about how many you killed. It's just doing what is right. Do you understand?'

'Okay, Grandpa,' said Michael as he turned his attention back to his toy soldiers.

'Pow! Pow! I got you, and I got you, too,' he enthused as he pushed over another six enemy combatants.

For my part, I was just happy to be released from the strain of explaining what to me was pretty simple. As a sniper in World War II, killing the enemy was my job. I left the lad to continue his war games and allowed my mind to drift as my eyes started to droop in deference to a desire for sleep. But as the fates would have it, sleep wasn't to be. All of an instant, I was jolted awake by a strange but somehow compelling sound.

'Hoot! Hoot!' came the call as a large grey owl swooped down to appear on the ledge of the open window.

'Wow! Granddad, will you look at that,' exclaimed the equally startled lad.

'Yes, it's come to pay us a visit,' I answered. 'Did you know, Michael, that owls are the signs of wisdom?' I didn't tell him the part about evil portents or messengers of death and wondered where that flash of insight had come from.

'Wow, I didn't know that ...' said the lad as he was interrupted by a call from his mother in the kitchen. He got up from the floor and went to dutifully attend the calling, leaving the room with a smile.

Moments passed while seconds turned into minutes as I again felt an irresistible calling to close my eyes. But this was different. It was more than sleep, more like I was being summoned. My breath seemed to deepen and my view of the room turned to shadow. I closed my eyes as the force was irresistible. It was then I saw the tunnel of light – like nothing I had ever seen before. Both beautiful and irresistible at the same time. I moved towards the light that surrounded my being in a comfort never known before. Then I heard it – like a hundred choral voices.

'Bring up the bodies. Bring up the bodies.' The words filled my ears and pierced my soul. I moved ever forwards, and still the sound never left me. Then, without warning, the veil of light parted to reveal the source.

They were waiting for me – all of them. Some I recognised, many I did not. All I knew was that they were the ones I'd killed in battle. I saw them as I had seen them through my scope. Many still had the look of agony on their faces as the bullet ripped into their flesh. Others looked surprised; some even looked content, thankful, even. I felt their collective confusion course through me like a tsunami as I drifted towards them – I couldn't stop. The sound of the crying voices filled me like a cacophony. There was no escape. I had to face them – face them all.

Before the tunnel of light had completely faded, I turned back to glance at the lounge room of my home one last time. My grandson, Michael, came bounding back into the lounge room, smiling at my body as he entered. His young face grew sombre as he noticed my head hanging limply to my chest. Michael gingerly approached and touched my arm, which was now dangling by the side of the chair. His mouth gaped open and his breath came in shallow urgent gasps.

'Mum, Mum,' Michael cried. 'Something's wrong with Grandpa ...'

CHAPTER 2

Michael, Age 9
Outback NSW, Australia, 1990

I couldn't quite work it all out. I guess as a nine-year-old boy, I was not expected to know much about many things. Everything seemed to be happening around me, not through me, although I do remember feeling really sad. It just didn't make any sense. One minute Grandpa was sitting in his recliner chair, and the next minute he was gone.

I tried touching Grandpa's hand, but that didn't seem to work. I couldn't wake him. After I called Mum – I guess she heard the urgency in my voice – she came running into the lounge room and immediately started to cry. She tried to wake Grandpa up too, but she couldn't do it either. After she stopped shaking him, she turned to me and grabbed me by the shoulders as tears fell down her cheeks onto her pretty floral dress.

'Michael, I need you to be a big boy now. Your grandfather has just gone to heaven, and I need you to be strong for me, okay?'

I nodded my head because I was a good boy and always did what I was told. I didn't really know where heaven was, but I figured that it must be a good place because my grandfather was a really nice man who I loved a lot. It didn't seem right though that he would leave without saying goodbye.

'When will Grandpa be coming back?' I asked. 'I want to finish playing my game of soldiers with him.'

Mum looked at me with love, but nothing much was making sense. The best Mum could do was cry some more and ask me to pack up my toy soldiers and take them to my room and play. Not wanting to cause any more trouble, I stacked all of my little make-believe soldiers into a plastic bag and walked slowly down to my room. As I moved down the corridor, the air seemed as if it had thickened somehow. It was totally different from before. The air felt heavy as if I was walking through molasses. Halfway down the passage, I stopped and turned around to look at Mum.

'Are you okay, Mum?' I asked as a tear squeezed itself from the corner of my eye.

'Yes, love,' she said with a sad smile. 'Just play in your room. Everything will be okay.'

I wasn't really sure what time it was, but later there seemed to be a lot of noise and commotion coming from the lounge room. I couldn't help myself so opened my bedroom door and went to see what was happening. Anyway, I was hungry and wanted to ask Mum for something to eat.

This time, as I walked down the corridor, the air felt really tense – still sad, but tense somehow. I just couldn't figure it out. It was somehow like the last five minutes of a really close football match. There were a lot of people standing around talking quietly, and I saw a trolley being wheeled outside by two ambulance people. It was covered by a white shroud and had something large and lumpy underneath it. The wheels made a grating sound as they rolled across the gravel in the courtyard, but I couldn't make out what the lump was. Mum was too busy for me to ask. She was talking to someone who had a stethoscope around his neck. He looked like someone I'd seen on television. You know, when they want an actor to look like a doctor, they always wear a white coat and a stethoscope around their neck. I could see that Mum had at least stopped crying.

After a short while, Mum shook hands with the doctor-person and saw me standing by the side of the door with my hands deep in my pockets, looking at the dirt stains on the well-worn carpet.

'Come here, Michael,' she said with a pinched smile.

With my hands planted firmly in the base of my pockets, I trudged slowly over to her, feeling the weight of each step like I had done something wrong. The carpet still looked particularly interesting, but even though I was only nine, I was smart enough to know that from one day to the next my world had changed – a lot.

'What was that?' I asked, pointing towards the ambulance people and the trolley.

I could see Mum starting to cry again but she quickly wiped her tears away with the edge of her sleeve.

'Those nice people are taking your grandfather to his final resting place,' she explained.

I looked at Mum in surprise. 'Do you mean that Grandpa is never coming home?' I stammered, only now really coming to grips with how my world had been turned upside down. Mum kneeled down and clasped me by the shoulders again.

'Michael, I'm afraid your grandfather won't be coming home anymore ...'

She said a lot of other stuff about Grandpa being in our hearts and when we looked up to the clouds, Grandpa would be up there, but I really didn't get any of that stuff. I guess Mum did her best to explain my first experience of death the best way she could, but it sure didn't make much sense. The only thing I knew was that it hurts – a lot. I missed my Grandpa. He had replaced my father, who had shot through when I was really young. I never knew him.

Matthew J. Cooper
Heaven

It wasn't so much that I didn't understand. I mean, the light I had followed and the tunnel I'd walked through were beautiful beyond description, but it just felt as if there were no more 'I'.

Having said that, I felt safe, loved, even. It was as if 'I' were a part of a bigger whole – an indescribable drop in a vast ocean of oneness droplets. I'd felt kinship before, but this seemed to be magnified by a factor of millions. It was as if we were all one, but separate none-the-less.

Yet, I could still see all of those dead people. I knew they were the ones I'd killed, even though many of their faces were unfamiliar. I could feel their pain. Each and every one. In war, the fact of the matter was that unless my orders were directed towards a specific target, I only ever saw the uniform – that was enough for me. Kill as many of the enemy bastards as I could – that was my job. If they had an SS emblem on their collar, more the better. They were the enemy – the evil ones. Krauts, Huns, Jerrys; the names were all different, but they meant the same thing. I tried not to look at their faces, and certainly not their eyes – that would have been too much of a distraction. My crosshairs were always focused on the exact same spot, just to the left of centre of their chest. I always aimed for the same spot. It was an instant kill, no suffering. They were the enemy, but I hadn't wanted any of them to suffer – none of them.

Even though my memory didn't serve much in recollection of faces, I now felt everything, everything they had felt when I had shot them. I could feel the agony I had caused as the one bullet – it was always only one bullet – ripped its way through the sinews and organs. Even though I hadn't kept a scorecard, there were hundreds of casualties. And when I say I now felt what they felt, it was more that I was experiencing it. Not suf-

fering, mind, just experiencing. Hard to describe, really. I was a
sniper, after all, not a Rhodes scholar.

I stood in total awe as these unifying experiences drew me into
the centre of what can only be described as a kaleidoscope.
Each part of the mosaic was an experience to be revealed –
pain, pleasure or pity. But mainly pain. Yes, it was a kaleidoscope, that's what it was. I saw everything in a moment. Felt
everything in an instant. I experienced what all my casualties
experienced as a result of that one bullet fired from my hands.
Mind you, it wasn't suffering. It wasn't as if I was on trial or
anything. I just felt what they had felt, experienced what they
had experienced as a consequence of my actions – that one bullet.

When I say I didn't remember the faces, well that's not absolutely true, there was one whom I remember. He was barely a
man, a mere boy filling out a man's uniform. A random target,
but one still young enough not to shave as the wisps of hair on
his chin and cheeks drew my attention from his uniform to his
eyes – his vivid blue eyes.

Of all who received the one bullet, I remembered this one's
eyes. I must have been closer to the target than normal. I could
kill from a long way away, that wasn't a problem. The scope
didn't lie. It told me everything I needed to know. I saw the bullet spin towards its objective like everything was in slow
motion. I saw the splash of red as the missile corrupted and
exploded his internal chemistry. I saw the light of life drain
from his eyes – his vivid blue eyes. I saw his mouth gape open,
but I couldn't hear the scream. After all, he didn't have much
time to scream. He died in an instant. But that wasn't all. There

was something else – something behind the silence of his open mouth and silent scream. I remember at the time hearing a vague something, but paid it no mind. But now was different; I heard it like it was uttered straight into my ear. No. It was more than that. It was straight to my soul. It wasn't hard to make out. 'My son. You've killed my son.' It was a mother's wail. She knew! But how did she know? She wasn't there.

I felt a wave of pitiless sadness fill my chest like an avalanche. If it were possible to shed tears in this place – wherever I was – I would not have been able to hold them back.

CHAPTER 3

Michael, Age 9
Outback NSW, Australia, 1990

I felt like I was covered over by a wet blanket of air as I stared at the never-ending field of tombstones outside the church. I shivered despite all my best efforts to remain strong, just like my mother had asked. I could hear the hoot of an owl perched somewhere out of sight, but which seemed determined to place its haunting tune over the people who had gathered to farewell my grandfather. The sound made me feel kind of sad and happy at the same time as we walked through the scary-looking doors of the church and down the aisle to the front row. The suit my mother had made me wear was a little small, and the studded collar pinched irritably at my neck. I did, however, do my best to stop fidgeting when Mum nudged my arm and raised her eyebrows at me.

Grandpa's medals made a soft jingle whenever I moved – even more so when we walked the distance from the church to the graveyard. The thick smell of incense from inside the church was still making my nose tickle, but I tried my best not to sniff like Mum asked.

This was a world totally new to me – the lights, incense and the many statues of a dead man hanging limply from a cross were so unfamiliar. Every experience was like something out of a book I had not read before. I watched as everybody filed past the open casket to take one last look at my grandfather's lifeless form. Many people were old just like him, and many wore medals that looked similar to the ones pinned on me. I sat as quietly as I could until Mum grabbed my arm and half pushed and pulled me up to the casket.

I had to stand on my tippy-toes to look over the edge of the casket at the still form of my beloved grandad. Mum was crying silently into her handkerchief and placed a red rose on his chest as a fresh flood of tears ran down her cheeks. I looked at my grandfather's motionless body. It made me think of the times I'd played on the floor in front of his chair when he'd fallen asleep. Although, this time, I couldn't hear his soft snoring. It was weird. I looked at Grandad then I looked up at Mum.

'Mum,' I said, as she was about to walk back to our seats. 'He's not there anymore. He's gone.'

Mum didn't say anything. She just looked at me funny and clasped my hand more firmly. She led me back to where we were sitting without saying anything more. I glanced back towards the still open casket just to make sure I was right. Nothing had changed. Grandpa didn't get up. He was gone.

As they were lowering the casket into the ground, the owl's song seemed to be heightened by a soft hum or gentle music, but I couldn't make out where it came from. It was as if beautiful music was drifting through the heavy mid-morning mist. *Maybe it was coming from inside the church*, I wondered. Mum had stopped crying, but she still looked really sad. It was then that I saw something. At first it was just out of the corner of my eye. I blinked as if it was a trick of the morning light through the mist. Then I saw it, over by the large oak tree just to the side of the grave. He was there. It was Grandpa. It was him, I was sure. But it wasn't him – if you know what I mean. He was standing there with his arms outstretched. His mouth opened as if he wanted to say something. His lips moved, and I was reading my name, but I couldn't hear any words.

I blinked again just to make sure I was seeing right and, yes, he was still there. The problem was, I could almost see right through him. He was there, but then again, he wasn't. I tugged at Mum's sleeve to get her attention, but the look she gave me was one I had not normally seen. Normally she was really nice, but this time I could tell she was angry.

'Mum, Mum, he's there, he's over there, beside the tree. Can't you see him?' I cried pointing to the spot under the tree.

'Who, son?' she replied irritably.

I looked at her strangely, not understanding why she couldn't see him. 'Why Grandpa, of course.'

I guess she couldn't help but look towards where I was pointing, but I knew she was angry with me because she tugged at my sleeve roughly and told me to stand still and not be so silly. I was a good boy, after all, so I stood as still as I could, but couldn't help sneaking glances towards the tree. Grandpa was smiling at me, so I smiled back at him when Mum wasn't watching.

I was startled back to the present moment when I heard the first thud of dirt landing on the wooden lid of Grandpa's casket. Although I tried to look sad on the outside just like everybody else, inside I was really smiling because I had seen Grandpa. I knew he was somewhere close by. It was just that I couldn't touch his hand or ask him to play toy soldiers with me. It wasn't ideal, but it would do, I reasoned. After the casket had been covered over with dirt and we all trod solemnly back to the cars, I turned to look towards the tree – but Grandpa wasn't there anymore.

Matthew J. Cooper
Heaven

I tried to tune out the wail of the enemy combatant's mother, but I couldn't. I knew I'd killed her son. I knew because his vivid blue eyes kept staring at me behind my own. The sound of his mother's crying was still resonating through my being. It was like it was a part of me. I couldn't shake it loose. But remember, it was like no more 'I', it was more like 'Us'. All of 'Us'. Like I was one with everything and everything was a part of me. It was terrifying and comforting at the same time. I was experiencing what others were thinking, saying and doing – what I had caused them to think, say and do. Yes, there was the pain, but I was not suffering. To me, it felt a bit like the pain you feel at the end of playing and losing a game of really tough football.

All of a sudden, I sensed something else – an irresistible feeling. A feeling that was both undeniable and enticing. I knew I had to go. I walked towards the light. From a distance I heard music – beautiful music. It gave me a feeling I can only describe as bliss. I knew I was safe. The force, the love was unconditional. Through the ethers, I could hear soft crying and the resonance of my name being spoken in reverence, but it was more than that. I could hear his soft voice ripple through my essence like a soothing balm.

'Grandpa, Grandpa, are you there?' I knew it was my grandson, Michael.

The light was too bright and anyway, this was not a seeing, it was more a feeling – a sense of oneness with someone. I stretched out my arms to him and could not resist a smile. I knew he was there, somewhere.

The light was all there was. It surrounded me totally, until there was no 'me' anymore. I was a part of this 'whole'. I had never been a religious man; I hadn't had time for any of that. I'd had a job to do. I'd been a sniper. It was what I had been made for. My job had been to kill the enemy, as many as I could, and I had been good at it. The very best! But I reckoned this experience of oneness was as close I was going to get to 'being' religious, I reckon.

One part of 'me' was still in the kaleidoscope. I was still remembering all that I had done. Now that I was 'dead', was I closer to God? I really didn't know who God was. Best I can describe this kaleidoscope thing is that it was a 'life review'. A bit like a snapshot of all life's events and experiences, but it wasn't so bad. It wasn't as if I were burning in hellfire or anything. It was more that I was experiencing 'things'. Things that I had done, things that I had done to others, how I made them feel – the consequences of my actions. At the very least it made me feel more at one with the 'whole' I was in.

Then, abruptly, I felt my being flying towards Michael. I could feel him. It was as if he were a part of me. He was calling my name. I could feel his sadness. I could sense his tears. I went to him – there was nothing else to do. I followed the light.

Michael, Age 9
Outback NSW, Australia, 1990

After we got home, Mum made everyone cups of tea and lots of sandwiches, but then, after they all left, the house felt vacant and eerily quiet. Nothing like what my home usually felt like. Mum was busy packing up and clearing dishes. I could hear the clang of pots and crockery through the door of my room. I didn't know what else to do, so I sat on the ragged old mat of my bedroom and opened my pack of toy soldiers.

I tried my best not to feel sad or anything, but when I got this picture in my head of Grandpa's empty recliner chair, I felt my chest heave and couldn't stop the deep sigh and tears that escaped. 'Grandpa, where are you?' I whispered as I sniffed loudly. I looked up quickly to see if Mum was watching from the kitchen. She hated it when I wiped my nose with my sleeve. But the clang of plates and dishes told me the coast was all clear. It was just that when I started to set up all of my toy soldiers in opposites according to who were the 'goodies' and who were the 'baddies', I started to really cry. I didn't know why, I just did. But I also knew how to fix it.

'Pow, pow, you're dead bad man,' I said through the tears as I pushed over the soldiers I had deemed expendable. 'Gotcha, right through the heart,' I said to another two as I pushed them to the floor.

But then, something really weird happened. I thought maybe it was the tears getting in my eyes, but maybe it wasn't. The last two enemy soldiers I had pushed over, the ones I had shot through the heart – they stood up again – on their own. They weren't dead after all.

I shook my head and wiped my tears with my sleeve. I felt a cool breeze blowing softly through my open window. It made the curtains sway silently, and I shivered involuntarily. From a distance, I could hear the 'hoot, hoot' of an owl perched somewhere in a tree outside. I looked up, but the light blinded me momentarily. From somewhere, I could hear my name being called.

'Michael, Michael, I am here. I am here.'

It sounded like Grandpa's voice.

CHAPTER 4

Michael, Age 13
Outback NSW, Australia, 1994

I reckoned Grandpa had been dead about four years now, and Mum wasn't home much anymore. I guess it was because she had to work a lot. I figured out that it takes a lot of money to run a household with a teenage boy in it. I had enough sense to understand that money didn't grow on trees, particularly when there was only one person to bring it in. You had to work for a crust. Grandpa taught me that. It was just that I couldn't quite figure out why Mum had to work so hard. She was always pulling extra shifts at the takeaway where she worked. Sometimes she didn't get home till really late.

Mind you, I didn't mind so much. I was used to fixing my own food. Now that I had turned thirteen, I was pretty self-sufficient, although I wasn't much of a cook. Sandwiches, baked beans or some other such limited offerings were usually the order. Anyway, it filled a hole, and I didn't seem to be hampered by any lack of proper nutrients. I was a growing boy. My feet had grown out of proportion, awaiting the rest of my body to catch up. If my size twelves were any indication, the rest of me was going to be six-foot-plus. Maybe that was the reason other kids got picked on at school, but not me. The bullies tended to pick on those smaller and less capable than themselves. Anyway, they knew that if they gave me a hard time, they were more than likely to confront a fearsome rage, as one lad, John, I think was his name, discovered. Mum had to take time off work to come to the school for that incident. And the sorry punk had two weeks off school for a fractured cheekbone.

Anyway, I suppose everything's relative. I mean, those other kids left me alone, and I was happy to *be* alone. I was quite capable of living in the world without some pimply-faced kid wanting to be my friend.

What was even better was that I didn't have to travel to school on the bus. I did this only once, and it really gave me the shits. I mean, all those noisy juniors mixed in with the 'older' seniors who thought their shit didn't stink. My legs were too big for the space between the seats. I had to dangle my limbs in the aisle. That too was a pain in the arse. I was quite happy to ride my bicycle to school. It was a hilly ride, but I didn't mind. At top speed, the wind in my hair made me feel like a superhero, and the exercise served me well as I watched my muscles grow bigger every time I flexed my biceps in the bathroom mirror. Other dudes went to the gym to muscle-up. Some played football. Me, I filled out just by doing what I loved doing as part of my daily teenage ritual.

My bike was my prized possession, and I looked after it like it was from the royal stables. The old shed out the back of the house wasn't used much, but it held enough old bits and parts to tend the needs of my bike. I used to go there often to do the essential service and repairs. I went there even more after Mum brought home my new stepfather a year or so ago. We got off to a rocky start him and me. I thought he was a bit of a wanker. Anyway, the ever-increasing arguments between him and Mum got on my nerves, so retreating to the peace and quiet of the shed proved a godsend.

Like I said, the shed was old and much in need of repair. The wind used to blow through the rotten boards and broken windows, particularly those facing west towards the scrub paddock behind the confines of our property. Those windows were so dirty you could carve your name in them. The windows facing east towards the road were a little better and did allow some perspective of the world going past.

This day, despite the bleakness of the weather – a chill factor of minus-something when I was riding – was like any other day until I got about halfway home from school. The front wheel of my bike started to shake like a busted shopping trolley. I had to walk the rest of the way home, lugging my backpack full of books along with my un-cooperative mode of transport.

When I arrived home, the house was quiet. It usually was. Mum was probably pulling an extra shift, and my stepfather was probably at the pub. I had the house to myself, so was quickly able to shove some food into my face before seeing to the needs of my bike – all without having to talk to anyone. Suited me fine.

I elevated the bike into the vice fit for purpose and set about trying to find the bits and bobs suitable for fixing the broken wheel. This was more than the usual puncture repair or seat adjustment. I needed some special tools to fix the buggered bearing. The light in the old shed wasn't the best, and it took me some time and numerous curses to scavenge what I needed. The jar on the top shelf, just to the left of centre, looked to contain the essential bearings. I reached high to remove the jar. It was then that I saw it. Covered in dust and in need of a good polish, was a wooden case. It looked to be just over a metre in length and felt about six or seven kilos after I reached up and brought it down from the top shelf.

I blew some of the dust off the lid and used a rag to remove the remainder of the grime before unclipping the latches and opening this slingshot to the past.

'Holy shit,' I exclaimed breathlessly as I lifted the rifle from its embedded casket.

It looked like a thing of beauty and felt like it belonged in the palms of my hands. It had a bolt action, and the telescopic range finder looked as good as the day it was made. I looked through the aperture but really couldn't see much within the confines of the old shed.

I heard the sound of my heart beating in my chest as I rubbed the all-wooden stock with the rag. It felt like I was caressing a thing of beauty. For some unknown reason, my dick even took a jolt to partial-erection ... now that really was strange. Time seemed to have come to a grinding halt. I barely heard the sound of tyres on the driveway as Mum came home from work. The weak lights in the shed didn't shine much into the gathering darkness outside as I quickly returned the rifle to its casket. I replaced it securely behind the other tools where I was pretty sure it was never going to be found by anyone but me.

Matthew J. Cooper
Heaven

Now, when I said I was with Michael that really didn't quite describe it. I was there but I was everywhere. It wasn't as if I had to be somewhere then went somewhere else – that wouldn't do the description any justice. It was more like where I thought ... I was. It was as if my thoughts were real and were the drivers of my experience – wherever I was. I knew that when Michael thought of me, I would know and I would be 'there'. Love was our bond – I could feel it. It felt like an invisible silver cord that connected us, heart-to-heart. We were not separate, only apart.

It was strange, I hadn't even given mind to the experience when I was alive, but now – here – my memory as a young teenager came flooding back in a wave. I remember when my dad first put the rifle in my hands. I couldn't help but feel a sense of awe, power even. I even remember getting a hard-on at the time and turning away from my father so he wouldn't see my embarrassment. I was sure I remembered my father smile knowingly at me. I guess he might have seen his own life reflected in his son's, but I wasn't sure about that.

The life review thing still continued as a work-in-progress. I knew it would. I was trying to make sense of my actions. After all, I had killed so many people. I had caused mothers to lose their sons. Fathers to mourn their offspring. That was all because of me. But I did it because it was right. It was war, and I was on the side of the right – at least that's what they told me, and I had no reason to believe otherwise. I mean, Hitler was some evil piece of work, wasn't he? Every shot I fired, all the blood I spilled was to make sure Hitler and his crazy notions did not take over the world as we knew it. 'Kill as many of the bastards as I could' and 'Kill or be killed' were always my mottos. Yet, now I could see the dead people. All of those I killed! Their cries pierced my soul like a dagger. How could this be so? I was only ever doing my job.

As these thoughts swirled around through my awareness, I could sense a presence – not that I could see it, mind. It was more a feeling of total love – of ultimate wellbeing. It felt like a warm blanket wrapped around to ward off a cold winter's eve. From out of this 'love' I heard a voice. It was as clear as the peal of a bell, like a voice-over in a movie:

'You stand not condemned for your actions. You cannot harm or damage the souls of those whose death you caused. Life is eternal. They are loved as you are loved. Those souls are like butterflies emerging from a cocoon. When you understand this, you too will have evolved. Only then will you hear the music.'

At one level the words brought me comfort, at another level, only more questions.

CHAPTER 5

Michael, Age 13
Outback NSW, Australia, 1994

I couldn't wait to get home from school the next day. It was as if the world had turned on its axis but time wasn't passing quickly enough. The drone from the teachers about algebra and where to place a comma were even more a mystery and even less a concern. All I knew was that sitting inside that rickety old shed was an object of beauty. I had no idea of its power, but I knew for certain that my future fate was intricately and intimately linked to that M40 secreted on the top shelf.

This time my bike didn't let me down, and I seemed to travel the distance between school and home in a time beyond my personal best. I knew without checking that Mum wasn't home, and I hadn't seen my stepfather for a few days. I think that was because he had this job driving rigs around the state. It was a relief to hear quiet within the house where Mum and I were able to move about our home without having to walk on eggshells. He was such a moody bastard, especially when he was drunk.

I dumped my backpack on the porch, parked my bike against the wall and made straight passage to the shed. My hands trembled slightly as I moved aside the concealments and reached for the case. I wondered whether my trembling hands were from anticipation or fear – I couldn't figure out which. Even so, I kept taking furtive glances towards the door, and my ears were pealed to the ever-possible sound of tyres on the driveway.

I made room on the workbench and placed the case down softly as if it were a sacred relic. But just at the same moment as the case touched the wooden bench, the light bulb sparked and the lights went out. Frightened the shit out of me, it did. With the shed now in total blackness, I had to quickly make things right so I could see what I was doing. It all took precious time and by the time I'd found a new globe and structured a better operating platform of light, I heard the familiar sound of tyres on the driveway.

'Far out!' was my frustrated response to the dismay at being interrupted.

'Michael, are you in there?' asked Mum as she slammed the door of her car. 'Come and help me with the groceries, will you, please?'

'Sure, Mum,' I grumbled as I scrambled to replace the case in its secret position. 'I'll be right there.'

Mum smiled at me with tired eyes as she saw me exit the shed and close the door securely behind me. She was always the same, Mum. You would never know how hard she was doing life, and I was always certain of the love behind her eyes. It never wavered. I picked up the remaining bags, made my way into the kitchen and started to help her unload and re-stock the pantry.

'When's he coming home?' I asked, preferring to replace his name 'the wanker' with a pronoun.

'If by 'he' you mean your stepfather,' replied Mum with a hint of ire, 'he'll be away until Tuesday. He's on a road-trip south.'

'Good,' was all I replied as I placed the milk in the fridge. Mum looked at me a second longer than normal, but obviously decided not to pursue the matter and instead asked me what I would like for diner.

We didn't say much over dinner, and the washing-up was mostly completed in silence apart from a few questions about school – that was until a strange question popped into my head.

'Mum, you know Grandpa?'

'Yes, of course.'

'He was in the war, right?'

'Yes, he was. Why do you ask?'

'Well, it's just that I've been thinking about him a lot, lately,' I replied.

'That's sweet, Michael. I miss your grandfather a lot. He was a good man.'

'Yeah, I know,' I said with a pause and a deep crease in my forehead. 'I've got his medals, but, whatever happened to his war stuff? You know, his uniform … or maybe a gun or something.'

Mum kept drying the last of the dishes as she pondered. 'I don't know. He never spoke about the war much, and I don't think he kept any of his war gear – at least not to my knowledge. I've never looked. Why do you ask?'

I turned to place a dish in the cupboard so I was sure she couldn't see my face. 'Oh, I dunno, I just wondered if he left anything behind, like photos or something?'

'There might be something in the attic. Why don't you take a look?'

'Yeah, good idea. I'll do that.'

The attic was full of dust and dim light. It had been missing human touch for many a long year. My footfalls left a trail on the floor from where I entered the roof hatch. *Geez*, I thought with a wry smile, *at least I'll be able to find my way out if I get lost.*

The place looked as if it were from a bygone era. The stuff that was stored away seemed to throw me back into a different time and a parallel world. It was like watching an old black and white movie on colour television. It gave me the shivers thinking about how our family's history lay unopened like a secret, despite its ever-presence in our lives.

I rummaged through boxes and crates, trying my best not to be distracted by objects that were not firmly in my crosshairs. It took some time, but finally, I managed to extract a box with my grandfather's name emblazoned on the side. It was a scuffed old leather suitcase with straps and a buckle that kept the contents secure from prying eyes. The anticipation was almost too much to bear, and my hands shook as they opened the slightly rusted buckle.

The opened lid revealed a whole new world that was a glimpse into a past life. I wasn't sure how long I was up there, because my reality seemed to lose all sense of time.

I lifted out the uniform first. It was in pretty good nick from what I could see, despite a livid stain on the front and a couple of needlework patch repairs. *Perhaps the stain was Grandpa's blood*, I mused as I placed the uniform to one side and returned my attention to the inside of the suitcase. The next thing I saw made me gasp like I'd been punched in the guts. The small arsenal of ammunition was like a present from Santa Claus. Without hesitation, I searched for something to wrap this unexpected treasure in and found an old towel to use. I was tempted not to press my luck and to close the case pending further investigations, but my eyes were drawn to a ragged leather satchel stashed under an old cap.

It wasn't locked but only tied with a strand of leather strapping, so I figured what was inside was not top secret. A lot old photographs, newspaper clippings and a well-worn diary fell to the floor as I shook the contents free from their long confinement. I flicked through the diary of handwritten notes and daily entries then figured I would be best served to explore these contents in the security of my own room. I was beginning to worry about being up in the attic so long and thought that I could even hear Mum calling my whereabouts. I took a quick look through the old photographs. Some looked really interesting, and I made a mental note to check them out later, but two in particular drew my attention.

The first was a picture of Grandpa receiving a medal from his commanding officer. He looked both resplendent and sombre at the same time as the medal was pinned to his chest. The other photo caused me to pause, but I wasn't sure why. Grandpa was standing with his arm around the shoulder of a colleague. Both were in uniform and both were smiling – obviously mates enjoying some fun as an interval to the horror of the war they both shared. I stared at the photo for quite a while, but couldn't work out what was so mesmerising. After all, it was just a photo of two mates in wartime. Then it hit me like a brick ...

The uniform that Grandpa was wearing. It was the exact same one that he left in the suitcase. I could tell by the series of patches on the left arm and upper thigh. But that wasn't all. I looked again at the uniform I'd placed on the floor. The stain was vivid across the chest, just to the left of centre. I turned the photo over and read the inscription,

'Barry and me' was written in a scribble, along with a date giving the photo a definitive point in time.

What was evident by its absence, however, was the stain – there wasn't one. I couldn't even begin to speculate why ...

I was so wrapped up in what I was doing I reckoned I switched off a part of my brain and didn't hear Mum's call to my whereabouts. I hastily reassembled all of the treasure trove into the towel and made my way back, retracing my footprints with a heightened sense of excitement.

Matthew J. Cooper
Heaven

I was still in this kaleidoscope thing and the images and sensations were like a perpetual cascade of my previous life's experiences. I didn't know how it happened because I still didn't know how things worked in this place, but I raised my hand towards one of the images in the mosaic. It was as if the image was calling to me. I couldn't resist. I touched it, and it opened to a breathtaking vista …

The grassy hillside was lush with the essence of divinity. The colours were more vivid than anything I had ever experienced. The gentle breeze caused the small flowers and grass to sway in gentle harmony with an unseen hand of grace. There was sunshine, but it was more than that … it's just hard to describe. A bit like your best picture intensely magnified a hundred times. I smiled to myself and wondered why I was here – wherever 'here' was. It didn't take long to find out. I saw him coming from a distance and knew exactly who it was because the memory shot through me like a bullet. It was Barry …

I remembered the day exactly as it unfolded. We were making our way through a lightly-wooded glen, en-route to our next killing zone with specific orders to kill a certain enemy commander. He was one of those Jerry-bastards who had caused us to lose too many good men because of his craftiness and strategic ability in evading our heavy artillery. It felt great having Barry by my side. He was a gifted spotter. We'd had plenty of kills together. I trusted his judgement, and he knew my strengths. He also didn't say much, so I knew that when he spoke it was worth listening to.

I heard the shot ring out before the damage was done – but I couldn't change history. I would have if I could. Barry's head exploded before my eyes as the sniper's bullet struck him just above his left eye. It all happened in slow motion from there. I saw his head disintegrate under the weight of impact. His blood sprayed everywhere, but it was the splatter of blood that hit the front of my uniform, just to the left of centre, that I observed in stark, slow-motion disbelief.

The next moments were a blur of self-preservation and automated reaction. In that instant, I knew Barry was dead. Instinctively my weight catapulted to my right leg to propel me towards the cover of a large tree, just as the next bullet rang clear. I felt its heat pass within millimetres of my left earlobe. I was alive, but it wasn't until the cover of nightfall that I could move again and retreat to the safety of our lines. I couldn't do anything about Barry. I had to leave him there; it was too dangerous. But my eyes kept straying to the splash of his blood on my chest ...

Both Barry and I covered the distance with a thought that was faster than the speed of light. Our mutual embrace was in recognition that we were both here – wherever 'here' was. We were both 'okay', and it was real. We kept slapping one another on the back and smiling like the best of mates usually do.

It filled me with joy to know that my mate Barry was alright. I didn't really know 'how' he was alright – he just was! After all, wherever we were, was real too. When I looked down at the space between us, I could see this silver cord stretch between our hearts. The cord kind of just expanded whenever and wherever we moved. It was almost the same as the one between Michael and me, but it was a slightly different colour, just not quite as vivid. This one between Barry and me had a slight bluish tint.

We looked at one another, knowing that it was time to go. We knew that we'd be apart, but not separate – if you know what I mean. We both knew that we could call upon one another whenever we chose ... or thought, more to the point. It was as simple as tuning into the silver cord between us– I knew that much.

CHAPTER 6

Michael, Age 13
Outback NSW, Australia, 1994

I wasn't sure how I did it, but I managed to get the old towel covering the arsenal and the photos out of the attic and into my room without Mum being the wiser. I knew getting the same into the sanctuary of the shed would not be a problem – I just had to wait. I slid the package under my bed and placed the two photographs securely on the wall next to my bed with a couple of drawing pins. The photos were strategically positioned so that I did not have to move my head from the pillow to look at them. Lucky, because just at that moment, Mum knocked on my bedroom door but came in before I could mouth a word.

'How did you go in the attic?' she enquired.

'Look,' I said pointing to the two photographs I'd placed on the wall. 'I found these two old photos.'

Mum strained over the bed to look at the old relics, and my heart skipped a beat when I thought of the ammunition inches from her feet.

'That's sweet, dear,' she said with a smile. 'Your grandfather was a fine-looking man, wasn't he? In fact, you're starting to look a lot like him when he was younger, don't you think?'

I squirmed a bit but had to agree with her conclusion. There was a budding resemblance.

'I wonder how that works?' she mused half to herself. 'You know, I remember your grandmother saying before she died that looks, talents and gifts pass genetically across generations, not from father to son, mind. They skip a generation, like from grandfather to grandson.'

'Is that right?' I said with a hint of surprise.

'Yeah, I guess so,' she replied as she turned to exit the room. 'And if you're as good a man as your grandfather, Michael, you will be well served as a man. Good night, son.'

I smiled back at her as she closed the door behind her. I took a last look at the two photos fixed proudly on my bedroom wall before I turned out the light.

When next I had a chance to get to the shed, it was like returning to the quiet safety of my bedroom. Both rooms were beginning to feel much alike. I was able to place the arsenal securely behind another concealed and unused piece of junk that hadn't been touched in a millennium. I didn't have the courage, as yet, to marry the arsenal with the action, although I had enough sense to ensure that the firing mechanism was empty every time I picked up the rifle. I had enough nous to know that I wasn't ready for that sacred union yet. What I was determined to do, however, was first to understand the mechanics. Perhaps, then, and only then, would I be ready to place the bullets where they needed to go.

I took the information I'd looked up and practised step-by-step how to dismantle and reassemble the rifle. I did it so often over the next few weeks that I was sure that I could do it in my sleep. I even went to the hardware store and bought the best oil to make sure everything was working like a well-lubricated machine. I figured if I was ever going to use this thing, I was damned certain that it was going to work properly – not blow up in my face. *No point getting dead from something you know not to do*, I thought.

What I couldn't resist, however, was the play-acting.

The old boards on the western side of the shed were so rotten that it was an easy task to make an opening to the world of shrub and vast paddock outside. I sat for hours on end with the rifle pointing towards anything that moved. I was out there so long sometimes I was almost caught by Mum when she came looking for me.

Fortunately, my ears had become well attuned to the sound of footfall on the grass and gravel around the shed. Anyway, Mum had no reason to doubt my intentions. She never tried to catch me out or anything. I guess she just appreciated that I liked to spend time in the shed fixing things, particularly when my stepfather was around. Anyway, I'd set my surrounds up so that I could quickly shelve the rifle in its secret spot then replace the hole in the wall with a plank if ever I were caught by surprise. I timed it once. It only took me ten seconds.

By the time I normally got home from school, the afternoon sun was making its way to sunset. That meant that the kangaroos, wallabies and scrub turkeys offered themselves in stark relief against the background setting. Sometimes a south-westerly breeze would pick up, and I was able to practise targeting on fast-moving tumbleweeds. God only knew if I would have hit them if it were for real, but I figured that my 'kill' ratio was seven or eight out of ten.

I often lay there so long my elbows were becoming red-raw with the scrapping on the shed floor. My shoulders and neck would ache because I was still for so long. By the end of an afternoon, I figured I'd 'killed' about three kangaroos, two bandicoots and one scrub turkey – all in my own mind, of course. But this taught me to watch and wait. Patience! Everything good happened if you just had patience.

I wasn't sure, but I think I was also getting pretty good at judging distances. The telescopic rangefinder was like another gift from Santa Claus. I always felt my pulse quicken a beat every time I had an animal fixed in the crosshairs. I squeezed the trigger, gently, mind you. It seemed to come so naturally.

'Pow! Gotcha! You're dead,' I would say to no one but myself. It kind of pissed me off when I saw the animal bound away after the surety of my imaginary kill. *Oh well, one day*, I thought, *I'll do this for real*.

Matthew J. Cooper
Heaven

That crying, that mournful wailing still wouldn't leave me alone. It surrounded me even when I was trying to think of something else. I knew who it was. It was the enemy combatant's mother. I knew because I'd heard her sobbing before – when I killed her son. Yeah, so I killed him. That shit happens in war. Yes, she felt sad because she had lost her son. Well, she wasn't Robinson Crusoe in that regard. But I didn't want to face her. I didn't want to deal with it.

I still didn't know much about how things worked in this place, but one thing I figured out was that there was no hiding. I couldn't sweep anything under the carpet and hope that it would go away. If there was an elephant in the room I was trying to ignore ... well, I couldn't. No doubt about it. And I had to look it straight in the eye. I watched my hand tremble slightly as I reached up into the kaleidoscope and touched the mosaic of the experience. All at once my vision exploded into darkness ...

I could hear the poor woman crying but I couldn't make out where she was. It was pitch dark and the air felt like a fetid wet blanket that smelled of unwashed linen sitting in a wash-basket for too long.

I reached my hands out into the darkness and inched forward, not knowing what I was walking into, or whether there was a forwards or even a backwards. Even despite this – it was

weird – I still felt safe. It was as if everything was okay. My
hand touched something and on impulse, I startled backwards.
A few more hesitant touches identified a door or portal of some
kind. There was no handle, so I pushed slightly to reveal what
God-only-knew was inside.

A dank, diffuse light met my vision, and putrid air corrupted
my senses. I had to hold fast to my nerve to stay and try to discern what this portal to the netherworld contained. At the same
time, the wailing became almost too much to bear. It was as if
someone had placed headphones over my ears and turned the
volume up really high. Then I saw who it was … it was the
mother alright. I knew because she had the same vivid blue
eyes as her son.

The poor wretch was curled up on the floor in a foetal position of what looked to be a caged cell of rusting iron bars.
Interestingly, I observed, the cage door was fully ajar. Her ragged and dirt-encrusted clothing made her look like a beggar-
woman. Her hair hung in filthy clumps and, on closer inspec-
tion, as my eyes adjusted to the vague light, I saw a livid scar
around her neck. She was still howling. The awful sound was
like the scrape of finger nails down a blackboard. It made me
almost want to puke – if I still had stomach contents.

She was rocking backwards and forwards while holding a
picture in her hand. I inched forwards to look at the picture,
but in my heart, I knew who it was. I could see the wisps of hair
on his chin and cheeks – and his vivid blue eyes. I couldn't help
it, my etheric stomach churned and I turned to dry-puke. It
was all I could do not to turn and run back out through the portal that led me to this vile place. But I stayed. I don't know how

long I stayed. I just did. It was as if I was fixed to a spot. I could neither move nor barely breathe. Then slowly she looked up at me … Her eyes were like pathways of brimstone, her face a mask to an eternity of pain.

'Franz, Mein Sohn,' she said as she returned to wailing and rocking backwards and forward.

I almost couldn't bear it. Without really knowing why, my hand reached out to her. I touched her on the arm that was holding the picture. All of a sudden, as soon as I felt the touch, the images of her life flooded into my consciousness.

She had thrown the rope around the central bearing of her living room and fixed the noose securely around her neck. The stool she stood upon looked as if it wouldn't hold her weight for very long, anyway. She clasped the photograph to her breast then kicked the stool asunder.

I gasped involuntarily as I watched her body twitch and convulse until it could twitch and convulse no more. The photograph of her son dropped from her rigid fingers and floated gently to the floor.

'Oh, my God! I am so sorry! I am so sorry!' I cried as I fell to my knees. 'I didn't know! I didn't know! I was just doing my job, that's all!' It was all I could mumble between the waves of confusion. I didn't know how long I was there – time really didn't seem to have any relevance. It didn't seem to exist. There was only the mother and I – and the experience of all her pain and sorrow. I felt her anguish like it was my own. It was overwhelming.

Eventually, the waves of torment seemed to abate – but the emotional anguish still lingered like a memory of a past horror.

I lifted my head into the thick gloom and glanced around to see that nothing had changed, except for the flicker of light. I saw the light – an irresistible light.

Then it was as if someone were speaking in my ear, but I was certain there was no one else around. I swear it. 'Follow the light. Move towards the light.' It was the sweetest sound I had ever heard. So that is what I did. I moved towards the light. As I did, I spoke into the ethers, 'I'm okay, but what about her? Will she be all right?'

The answer to my question flooded the very essence of my being like a tsunami. 'She is loved, eternally. She will see the light, eventually.'

In an instant, I was back inside my kaleidoscope ... *Geez, thank God for that*, I thought, *it's almost starting to feel like home.*

CHAPTER 7

Michael, Age 15
Outback NSW, Australia, 1996

You know, it's like no plan ever survives contact with pre-determined destiny. I had every best intention to start loading the gun and setting about rifle-shooting practice for real during the forthcoming school holidays. I figured Mum would normally be at work until all hours. My stepfather would be on the road to somewhere, and I'd have the house to myself. I'd have whole days to just 'go bush' well out of earshot of any in the local community.

We were about ten minutes' drive from what we called our nearest town, if you could call a hotel, one convenience store, a few takeaways, a café and a pawn shop a town. Not to mention the abattoir on the outskirts. It took another six hours hard driving to get to the nearest city. Out here, however, where the

sun didn't set on the never-ending plains, we had enough farm-
ers and local hunters around to ensure that any gunshots were
not identified as my own. I had it all figured out. I'd even
amassed a rucksack full with enough provisions to see me
through a day of hiking.

That was until the world turned off its proper axis, again.

It was the first day of the last week before the extended
Christmas holidays. Despite everything else, I'd managed to
pass (just) all of my subjects. To this day, I still don't know how,
given my limited concentration in class and lip service to external study. Anyway, no matter! Mum was happy that I
passed, and I didn't give a shit what my stepfather thought.

The day seemed to start much like any other. School came
and went. I managed an hour or so 'fixing things' in the shed
until Mum arrived home and the large rig that was my stepfather's second home turned up an hour later.

Mum was cooking dinner while my stepfather was sitting in
the armchair in the lounge. He had a preference for the one my
old grandfather used to sit in. Perhaps that's one of the reasons
I didn't like him, I'm not sure. His sweat-stained singlet covering his fat belly made him look like he'd eaten a bowling ball
and failed to digest it. He was watching the news and railing
about 'wanker' politicians at the same time as downing beers at
a speed normally reserved for a football match.

Mum did her best in the kitchen. She wasn't a bad cook and
the meat and three vegetables she served far exceeded my usual
hash of baked beans or sandwiches. She also did her best to

keep the stilted conversation across the dining table civil enough. She asked how school was going and my 'well-read' stepfather added that all education was a load of shit. 'Get your hands dirty. That's what a real man does,' were the limits of his intellectual prowess between another three cans of lager.

Anyway, Mum smiled as I asked permission to leave the table and wash up my own dishes. I was a good lad, after all. I didn't want Mum to have any more work to do than she normally did. My stepfather just belched loudly and went back to his recliner chair in the lounge without helping. Oh, he helped himself to another beer, that was about it.

I trudged back to my room and closed the door. I felt a bit knackered so lay down on my bed and just stared at the photos on the wall. It was then that the raised voices started.

I couldn't quite make out what the argument was about, but it seemed to grow exponentially across a narrow timeframe.

Raised voices and angry accusations I could deal with, but the slap and sound of broken glass froze me to the spot. It was as if I'd been transfixed. I didn't know what to do. I didn't know how long I stayed that way, and the pillow over my head didn't work. After the initial sound of the slap and crash, the air in my room seemed to carve a hole in itself. That was until the next slap and the sound of Mum screaming – that made me jump up.

I yanked opened my bedroom door and within a few giant strides I was in the lounge room.

I didn't know where it came from – the fury seemed to surface from somewhere deep inside me. It felt like a raging inferno that spewed molten heat and lava from the mouth of a volcanic crater. When I saw my bastard stepfather standing with his fists clenched over my prone mother, well – that was the trigger. Mum was crumpled on the floor up against the wall. She was cowering under her arms with blood pouring from a cut above her left eye. The son of a bitch was breathing heavily with a look on his face like a triumphant boxer over his defeated prey.

I didn't think – I just sprang. I felt a couple of blows land somewhere on his head. I wasn't sure where. I didn't really care. My arms just kept flailing – that was until he landed one – a punch right to the side of my left cheek. It knocked me sense-less, and I hit the floor like a sack of potatoes. I don't know much about what happened after that. The next morning was the great revealer ...

Mum and I were in the kitchen. There were so many elephants in the room it was difficult to know where to start, or even if we could start. It was uncomfortable. She was busying herself to fuss about making me breakfast, and I just sat there looking profoundly at the tablecloth with the bruise under my eye throbbing like a bitch. Mum told me that I'd been knocked un-conscious and that she was worried sick when she couldn't wake me up. She said that it took more than a few minutes and a cold compress on my check before I came to. When I looked at the livid cut above Mum's eye I knew just how wonderful a person she was. How she managed to get me to my bedroom in the state that she was in, I'd never know.

It was strange because as she was telling me this I kept get-ting these flashbacks of my grandfather. It was like he'd been with me somehow. I kept seeing myself holding his hands. It was weird, and I couldn't quite grasp it. It was like a thought out of reach, but I knew it was there. It almost made me smile, but I couldn't because my face hurt something severe.

I guess Mum must have called in sick at work, and she told me that she'd spoken to the school to say I wouldn't be in today, and probably not for the rest of the week. While I wasn't overly concerned about the prospect of showing my cruelly bruised cheek and left eye to the school population, not going to school saved me from having to explain myself to people I didn't care about.

I watched Mum move about the kitchen cooking eggs and making toast. The bruise and cut on the side of her face were even more livid than my own. There were so many unanswered questions spilling through my mind, I could hardly make sense of any of them. I guess, after I'd looked at the table long enough, the biggest question was, 'Where is the son of a bitch?' The feeling rose from my gut just thinking about it. It was like a furnace, an uncontrollable fire that wanted to spew forth no matter the consequences.

'Mum,' I said, as the words grated across my reluctant vocal chords.

She turned to me as she switched off the flame on the stove. She couldn't help herself. She was trying really hard, but she couldn't help it. Tears burst forth and her normally placid demeanour shattered into shards of broken dreams and ragged expectations.

'Oh, Michael, I'm so sorry. I'm so sorry. I didn't mean for it to be this way.'

Her apron found another purpose as she lifted it to wipe the tears from her cheeks and red-blotched eyes.

I wasn't much for hugging or anything. In fact I couldn't remember the last time I hugged my mum, but I knew what to do in this case. I got up from my seat and hugged her until her tears stopped flowing and her gasps for breath returned to some semblance of normal.

'It'll be all right, Mum. It'll be all right,' I kept repeating.

Eventually, she shook herself back to a resemblance of the mother I knew. Anyway, the hug was starting to get towards the embarrassing. I turned to resume my seat, and she to put eggs on my plate.

'Mum,' I said finally finding the courage to ask my most pressing question. 'But what are we gonna do now? What about the son of a ... Him?'

You know that I said before how the world turned upside down ... well, it did again.

'It's okay, son. The bastard's gone. I kicked him out. I told him I was going to call the police and have him arrested.' She tried her best to smile as she told me the next part. 'I think the weak son of a bitch panicked when he knew I was for real.' She moved over beside me and ruffled my hair gently, 'Nobody's going to hurt my little boy and get away with it. I can tell you that now.'

What a mum! Tough as nails, soft as silk and as strong as a lion. Everything was back to normal. Whatever normal was. Those simple words! Four words that realigned the universe: 'I kicked him out.' This changed everything.

It's hard to express how I felt at that moment and even harder to describe what I did. I guess it all comes back to being a teenager. The best I can do to explain things is through what I said. 'It'll be all right, Mum! We'll make it right, just you and me. Don't worry.'

Every boy-child has to become a man someday, doesn't he? This was my time. I knew because something had 'clicked' inside of me. It was my time to 'step up to the plate'. I didn't say it to Mum, but that's what I thought. I was fifteen years old ... it was my turn to bat. But I stayed silent about my rage. I just rationalised it as something to do with protecting my mum. Anyway, I was only a teenager, not that psychiatrist-bloke Sigmund Freud they'd told me about in school. The best I could figure was that if anybody ever tried to hurt my mum again, I'd be happy to open the door to my rage. Oh, and something else ... the other thing that kept bothering me was the fact that, 'I couldn't fight for shit'. I was a pussy-full-of-fire. I was going to learn how to fight. For me, it was a simple equation:

Rage + Fight-skills = Victory.

Anybody that was going to mess with me was going to face 'The Equation'.

Oh, and by the weeks' end, all of the bastard's stuff had either been dumped in the trash or sent to help those in need. That was kind of cool, too.

Matthew J. Cooper
Heaven

To say that I was back 'where I belonged' really does describe things. The thing was, I was perfectly aware that I was totally loved. It also wasn't so much a 'me', it was more like 'all'. I was a part of everything that was. It was a weird feeling, but that's what it was, a feeling. Even more than that – it was as if I 'knew'. Something akin to a deep-rooted understanding of the way things are.

As I basked in the feeling, thinking that everything was pretty much like bliss, I felt a strange tugging on my chest. I looked down in surprise to see one of those silver cords. It was shining vividly and calling me to action, like an unanswered ringing telephone. It was Michael's cord – he needed me. He was in crisis. I just knew it. I felt his anger. It was like a raging inferno being let loose. I knew – I'd experienced the same thing when I was 'alive' as a flash of 'that' door to my own labyrinth of memories whizzed by unrestrained. It was the place I never wanted to enter. I never did, but remembered the door opening ajar of its own volition a few too many times but couldn't confront what was inside. I just knew this was one of those times for Michael. My hand went directly to the cord, and I went plunging into a brightly coloured matrix ...

I couldn't 'see' him – I wasn't able to pierce that great veil – but I could 'feel' his life's presence and I knew he had lost consciousness. What I did 'see' was his 'soul' hovering above his body. While his physical body lay unconscious on the floor, his 'soul' was floating, kind of lost, not knowing what to do or where to go. His soul didn't know, but I did! I didn't know how I knew, I just did. I reached out to his 'hovering soul' and took him by the hands. It was a gesture in total abandonment to the experience of love. I saw in his 'soul's eyes' an instant recognition. He knew it was me, and he knew he was safe.

I didn't know where my words came from. It were as if an angel was speaking in my ear and I was merely reciting dictation. I held Michael's 'soul-hands' fast and gazed into his eyes.

'It'll be all right, Michael. We'll make it right, just you and me. Don't worry.'

These words had their desired effect because he looked at me and smiled. I watched with joy as his soul 'flew' back into his body, and I saw his body twitch as his returning essence brought it back to life.

My job was done – for the minute. I knew he would be okay. It was time to return to where I belonged.

CHAPTER 8

Michael, Age 15
Outback NSW, Australia, 1996

It was the first day of the school holidays. I couldn't wait. I knew the day would come. The bruise on my face was now but a figment of its former self. The vivid purple bruise had morphed into a putrid yellow, but I really didn't mind. It was only a matter of time before it all went away. I knew Mum's bruises had also started to fade because I saw less and less of her the more she returned to work and made up the shifts she'd missed. I guess women can do more with makeup than boys can.

It was an amazing thing, really. Bruises faded, but memories didn't. The events of that night kept swirling through my brain. I couldn't stop them. It was like every time I had time to myself, I would see the bastard's ugly face in front of me. I could feel my fists pounding into his skull and see blood spewing from his mangled nose and eyes. At least that's how it was in my daydreams. I knew it wasn't 'okay' to be reframing the events of that night in such a way, but I couldn't help it. Every time I saw myself hitting him in the face, I felt a fire, like a burning anger, seep into my being from somewhere unknown. The only way I could put a temporary halt to these images of blood and carnage was to go to the shed.

The shed was my oasis, and it wasn't as if I hadn't picked the rifle up before. I'd done it a thousand times, but this time was different. This time, when I picked up the M40, I felt its power reverberate through me like a bolt of electricity. It was as if the rifle was helping me transform a living nightmare into a bearable reality. I touched the rifle's sleek contours and felt its weight. It was as if an authority far greater than I had ever known had entered my body and was starting to overtake me. I could feel, deep down, that I was dangerous, more potent than ever before.

I was a teenager! I'd watched a lot of television and some pretty violent movies and video games. I'd seen a lot of shoot-ups, heists and murders where guns were the central means of conflict resolution. Movies were the place where disputes seemed inevitably to be resolved down the barrel of a gun. I knew all that shit wasn't real, but it was raw, and I empathised with the good-guys and railed against anyone seeking to antagonise the weak or vulnerable.

I knew that I was a reasonably rational kid. I didn't suffer from depression. I wasn't confused, deluded or overly fearful. It was just that the gun had a way of making me feel I was something more than 'myself'. I knew the M40 was a work of art, but I didn't see it as sacred. It wasn't sacrosanct, but it did have a way of making me feel more powerful than I actually was.

Matthew J. Cooper
Heaven

It was when I was staring absent-mindedly at the multi-faceted colours and images in my kaleidoscope that I remembered his words quite clearly, 'You have done your country a great honour.' That's what the captain had said as he pinned the medal to my chest. I recalled thinking at the time that I was only doing my job. The one I was trained for. It was more than that, though. The reality was that I'd been conditioned, ever since my father placed that first rifle in my hands. Hey, the first time I fired it – at a tin can, I think – made me feel like a God. The first time I shot a kangaroo gave me a hard-on. *Anyway*, I had mused, *if something good came out of all that conditioning, well then it couldn't be too bad*. I mean, if everyone were given a medal for doing 'what they were trained to do' and 'just doing their job', they'd have to print a lot of medals, wouldn't they!

The captain's face was firmly implanted in my mind, so I reached into my life review 'kaleidoscope' with the memory implanted in my awareness ... I had no idea where it would lead. Perhaps, if I had have known, I probably wouldn't have gone there. I may well have been better to have left the memory well alone. But, that wasn't how these 'review things' worked in this place ...

I knew the captain to be a good man, a moral man. I figured that was probably the best you were ever going to get in wartime, and from somebody 'high up the ladder' as well. Truth be known, I was never much for tipping my hat to anybody. Just didn't seem right. We were all born equal as far as I could figure. But, I guess, someone had to give the orders. Someone had to lead the troops and that sure as hell wasn't me. I was no leader. I was just a common grunt, albeit with a particular talent for killing the bad guys. What was the score, now? Oh, I didn't know. I never did count.

When the captain called me to the command post, I knew something big was up. To be summoned like that meant that I was being called on for something out of the ordinary. His drawn face and sharp, nervy movements attested to a mind full of the weight of responsibility, or burdens of guilt. I saluted, but he ignored the protocol preferring to get straight down to business. It seemed that the enemy had found a new way of trying to win the war, and after the captain told me what was happening, I was pretty sure I was going to be the implement of their demise. The job was right up my alley.

Improvised explosive devices, or IEDs as they were called, were now all the rage. But, as far as I was concerned, to detonate a bomb that would rip the legs from our unsuspecting troops and cause untold damage to the frail human condition was just not playing the game by the rules. I'd seen enough corpses, maimed bodies and hu-

man carnage being littered back from the front line to know that the human body was not designed to deflect shrapnel. Something had to be done ... and I was just the man to do it.

We had plenty of good intelligence and knew exactly who the mastermind of the operation was. The problem was, we had to get to him and we had to do it right. The captain passed over the mongrel's photograph. Shit! I thought. He looks just like a regular guy – apart from the uniform he was wearing. I mean, he could have been a regular guy you passed on the street if it hadn't have been wartime. He certainly didn't look any smarter than me, and he didn't seem to have any external indicators or visible scars that would contort him from proper standards of morality – even in wartime.

I planned the kill immaculately – just like I always did. I knew where he would be, when he would be there and what I had to do. Thank God for the partisans; it was all good intelligence.

Days later, I set up the ambush. Then I waited. I was good at that, but this wasn't going to be my regular type of kill. This one was close range. No need for an M40 on this job. This was dirty work. A small calibre Colt .32 pistol would do the trick. That's all I needed. Oh, and a bloody big knife.

My cover was perfect. I didn't mind the dirt and rough coverage of rubbish and rubble. Those slight discomforts caused me no mind, and my memory banks were alive and well as I waited. I liked to wait.

The three arrived at the appointed hour – two bodyguards and the target. They had no idea what hit them. I sprang from the cover like a crouching tiger stalking its unsuspecting prey. Two shots from the Colt were all it took to reduce the odds to one-on-one. My target's bodyguards didn't even have time to twitch. The kills were fast. A bullet each to the mid-forehead did the trick. They both hit the dirt like wasted sacks of potatoes. No time to ponder the meaning of life for those cretins. That left just him and me – with the odds certainly in my favour.

I kept my eyes on his, but much to his surprise, I replaced my Colt back inside its holster. At first, I could see his terror. He was shitting himself. Then, after I unsheathed the knife – and it was a big knife, so he knew exactly what the state of play had become. It was him against me, right against wrong, the just against the un-just, no quarter given, none shown.

We squared off, but I knew I had his measure. I was in my 'com-fort zone' and he was well on the extremity of his. He had a knife, not an IED. I had a knife, not a gun, but it was an extension of my-self, an addition to the whole. It wasn't some errant improvised weapon detonated from a remote location. It was like an extra limb. I saw it in his eyes. He knew I was going to win. I watched as he fingered the iron cross that was fixed between the collars of his uni-form ... then we came together.

Outwardly, it could perhaps be viewed as a melee, but for me, it all happened in slow motion. I saw everything in stark relief to it-self. I knew his moves an instant before he was going to make them. It couldn't have taken more than a minute before he was prone on the ground, his knife-wielding hand shattered beyond repair and a deep twelve-inch gash across his chest.

My full weight on his gasping and heaving torso and the big-arse knife held across his throat told him that he was soon to add a notch to my scoreboard. I looked into his eyes before the execution. It *was funny, normally I never thought of anything before I pulled the trigger. But this time was different.*

'Why?' I said to him with a clarity that he didn't seem to understand as his forehead creased in confusion. 'You bastard! You killed and maimed our soldiers. You didn't fight fair. How could you do that?'

I'm not sure if he understood my words properly, but I'm certain he got the gist of meaning. Once again, he mouthed words that sounded a bit like, 'Gott im Himmel'. Then he looked at me with eyes full of their last earthly visions.

I asked 'why' again but his words were a bit difficult to follow, although I understood him clearly enough. 'Because you are vermin. I am fighting for the glory of the fatherland. You scum must all be wiped from the earth.' I think he said, 'parasites' after that, but I may have got that confused because of his accent.

Now, I was a simple man. I was not religious, but I knew right from wrong, so the next bit I did on purpose. I went to 'that' room in my mind and opened the door. You know, the one that held the raging inferno. I felt the comforting heat spread through every atom of my body. Then I looked at the knife in my hand and watched it bite deep into his exposed throat – just above the iron cross. Mind you, the kill was quick. I didn't let him suffer. That wouldn't have been right.

I wrote about this 'kill' later in my diary when I got back to camp. It bothered me a bit. I couldn't sleep for a couple of nights. Maybe that's when the nightmares started? Not sure why really, they just did. I guess, someday, at some other time, someone will read the words I'd written. I suppose that whoever reads them might

make sense of this shit-box of a war and what it does to good people.
But it will take someone smarter than me to that work out ...

It was all over in the blink of an eye. The memory was finished.
I was back where I belonged, but with a difference. I could feel
'that' comforting presence again. I didn't know who or what it
was, just that it was warm and full of love and compassion. But,
again, I couldn't see, I could only feel and hear as the words
echoed through my soul.

'You are not doing the will of God when you harm one another. There is always a higher way,' said the voice. 'Know this
and you too will evolve. Only then will you hear the music.'

Michael, Age 15
Outback NSW, 1996

I was lying on my bed staring at the ceiling. Nothing had been
out of the ordinary for the day. Mum had been a bit late home,
but that was normal. I'd fixed my own dinner. It tasted like
crap but that too was par for the course.

But then, it was as if someone or something was speaking in
my ear. A picture of Grandpa appeared in my head. I had this
sudden urge to look in his old diary. I followed the instinct and
reached under my bed to pull out the leather satchel and released the ties. My hands were trembling slightly as they
loosened the binds. The book fell open on the bed.

I felt a bit stupid, I mean, there was nothing to be nervous about, was there? I turned the book over to the opened page. The page was a bit dog-eared and had a couple of dirt smears from wayward fingertips. It was a handwritten diary entry much like many of the others. I read the inclusion:

Killed a man today, a man who seemed much like any other, except he wasn't. He killed our men - maimed them, he did. But now the bastard's dead. I killed him with my own bare hands. The captain said I was going to get a medal for what I'd done. Seems a bit strange really, because I was just doing my job.

The problem was, the enemy soldier said something to me, just before I cut his throat. He said that I was a parasite. Put the wind up me a bit. I mean, he's the one who should be sent to find out if there's a hell, right? The bastard planted bombs that killed our people. He also said that we were all vermin, so we must all be killed. Doesn't seem right to me. I mean, if I'm right, how come he thinks he was right. There can only be one right, right?

Anyway, I cut the bastard's throat ... he won't be killing any more of our boys anymore that's for bloody sure!

I read the words over and over until I knew them by heart. Then I remembered what Grandpa had said to me when I was really young. He told me that when you go to war it's about killing as many of the bad people as you can. Kill or be killed. That's what he said, I remembered.

I fell asleep with the open diary on my lap.

CHAPTER 9

Matthew J. Cooper
Heaven

There was no escape. It was like an irresistible urge, an itch that just had to be scratched. The piece of mosaic in my kaleidoscope shone in full force. I just had to touch it. The brightness was almost blinding. It created a compulsion – I had to go there. My hand reached up into the matrix of colour, sound and sensation. The experience, the memory flooded my being like a tidal wave ...

I was safe behind secure lines, miles from the frontline. The word on the grapevine was that we were taking a severe beating, the loss of

life enormous, and the cost of men, their blood and equipment be-yond the pale of expectation. I was on so-called, 'r'n'r', but had noticed over the past days that the returning traffic of ambulances and litter-bearers had exceeded even our abhorrent standards. An-yway, I stationed myself in the far corner of the pub, as close to the fireplace as I could squeeze without having to encumber or encoun-ter anyone else.

My schooner of beer was almost empty, and I was wondering how to get a refill without giving up my spot when the dilemma was solved for me. The boy-soldier was barely a man. I knew the age of enlistment to be eighteen or over, but if this lad was a day over the pre-requisite, then I was a poor judge of age. He was barely old enough to shave and not old enough to swear.

'Can I buy you a beer?' he asked politely as he motioned with his chin towards my empty schooner.

I looked at him with what can only be described as 'shit, do I have to', but then my better graces came to the fore and nodded ac-ceptance to the kindness of his offer.

He returned with two full schooners, placed them somewhat nervously on the small round table and took up the vacant seat be-side me.

'What's your name, Private?' I asked just to be friendly and be-cause it was the only thing I could think to ask.

'Jonathan, sir! Private Jonathan Baker, rifleman, 1st Infantry Division.'

I picked up my beer and took a small sip to make it last longer. 'Thanks for the beer,' was the next best thing I could say before a pregnant silence formed a solid wall between us.

As he picked up his glass to take a rather liberal swig, I noticed that he was holding his right wrist with his left hand to stop it shaking.

'Are you right-handed?' I asked out of curiosity.

'Yes, sir. Why?'

'Because, Private, you better learn to stop your hand from shaking before you shoot. That is, if you want to hit anything.'

The boy looked down at his hand for a few overly long moments.

'Sorry, sir, I can't help it.'

We both took another swig from our respective schooners and pondered whether we both wanted to breach the gulf into the expanse of no-man's-land between us.

'Your first time at the front?' I asked with some hesitation.

'Yes, sir, I was billeted in yesterday; my company's being shipped to the front tomorrow morning.'

I reached for my schooner again and tried without success to stop my next question from forming, but I couldn't help it.

'Ever killed anyone?'

The boy's eyes took on a rather petrified guise, a bit like an uninitiated Roman gladiator about to enter the arena for the first time.

'No, sir.'

I watched again as he held his right wrist with his left hand to pick up his schooner. 'Have you?'

I looked at the barely-out-of-nappies lad with a look somewhere between understanding and incredulity.

'Yeah, lots,' I replied, 'but I don't keep score.' I again reached for the security of my glass.

'How does it feel?' he mumbled into his now half-empty beer.

'How does what feel?' I replied with the pretence of ignorance.

'To kill someone, I mean.'

I looked at him sharply but understood intuitively that a boy-soldier was entitled to a semblance of wisdom.

'Look, it doesn't pay to think much about that shit. The fact of the matter is we're at war. In war, it's either kill or be killed. They are the enemy ... Understand?'

He reached for his glass, but his hand still shook.

'Yes, sir, I guess so, but ...' he said with hesitation.

'Look, Private,' I said more firmly than I should have. 'No, buts. You shoot. You kill, before the enemy does it to you. You got that?'

'Yes, sir,' he replied, somewhat more resolutely.

There was a quiet background hum from the other patrons in the old pub, and the firelight danced light and dark between the movements of people and muted conversations. I watched as the boy took his still trembling right hand and retrieved something from the inside pocket of his jacket. It was a letter. His hand still shook as he passed it across to me. I looked at that letter without touching it for more moments than I should have.

'Sir, please, would you mind? It's for if I don't make it back. It's for my mum.'

I looked at the letter in his outstretched hand, but was still averse to touching it.

'Give it to her yourself. When you get home,' I said with as much conviction as I could muster.

The air between us was well warmed from the fire, but it suddenly seemed to carve itself into blocks of ice.

'I don't think I'll be coming home, sir ...' he said.

I don't know. It was weird, his saying that. I'd never thought about things like that. I'd never figured anything, other than 'kill or be killed' and 'get the bastards before they get me'.

I took the letter and placed it in the left inside pocket of my jacket, all the while mumbling something about 'being careful' and 'following orders' or some such shit.

That was enough. I'd had enough amber fluid. Anyway, I suddenly felt an impulsive urge to sleep or piss or something. I thanked him for the beer and made my way back to the comfort of my quarters without any further need to converse, think or be wise to the uninitiated.

Three days later, I was walking along the mud-encrusted roadway that ran through the middle of our encampment. The northerly was biting a hole through everything it touched, and I felt the depths of my pockets as I watched dispassionately from the sidelines as a bunch of soldiers returned from the frontlines. They all looked much the same – ragged, exhausted, with a faraway, haunted expression. The soldiers were followed by the litter-bearers.

I didn't call for it; I didn't ask for any kind of divine intervention, but the brisk northerly had other ideas. I was watching as one of the litters passed by at the same time that a gust of northerly decided to blow the sheet from the face of the body on the litter ... It was Jonathan! Somehow I knew it would be.

My hand made an involuntary motion to my chest, just to the left of centre. I felt the letter to his mum burn a hole straight through my chest. The shame I felt was palpable – I hadn't even bothered to move the letter to a place of security, nor even given it a second thought.

I felt instant rage rise up from 'that' room in my mind again. Shit! I didn't even have to open the door. It just came out. I marched straight into my CO's tent and asked for more orders. I remember he looked at me strangely knowing that I had two days of unused leave remaining. Then I marched straight towards the mail dispatch tent.

I felt the experiences as if I had been there, again. But the vivid memories parted and I turned abruptly when I felt a presence, a strong divine presence, approach. I had to shield my eyes from the light. It was blinding, but it was more than light; it was ... radiance. I felt overwhelmed. Overwhelmed by a feeling of grace from a being of light.

'Don't you recognise me?'

I knew the voice and peered keenly into the light from which he appeared. Confusion turned to recognition.

'I ... Is it really you?'

'Hello, sir,' he said with a smile that was like no other I had ever seen. It was like being smiled at by a God.

'Jonathan, I, it is good to see you ...' I mumbled.

He kept looking at me with that divine expression and tilted his head slightly in evidence of my confusion.

'I couldn't do it, sir,' he said.

'Couldn't do what, son?' I replied still bemused and over-whelmed.

'I couldn't kill them, sir. I couldn't shoot anyone. I tried ... I aimed, I had an enemy target in my sights, but I couldn't shoot.'

'But, you're here, I mean, you must have been ... killed,' I mumbled devoid of further comprehension.

'Yes, sir, I was shot. They saw me. I couldn't shoot ... but they could – right in my heart.'

'But, why, I don't understand? Why didn't you shoot first – just like I told you?'

'It's okay, sir, you will understand soon. When I aimed, when I looked through my scope, I saw what was real. I knew in that instant that I could not shoot, and I knew why.'

'But, why? I still don't understand ...' I replied.

'Sir, when I looked through the scope, I saw a face, I looked at his face ... it was my face.'

I felt my mouth open and close without being able to form proper sounds.

'Do you hear the music, sir?' he asked as he looked at me with what can only be described as the purity of love.

I strained my ears, but could not hear anything apart from his words.

'No,' I mumbled.

'You will. You will, soon,' he responded with a radiant smile. Then, he lifted his hands in a gesture of friendship. 'I have to go now. They are calling me. I have to return. That is the music – they are the music.'

I tried to stop him leaving, but I couldn't. For some unknown reason, I stretched my hands out to his. 'Can I come with you? Please!' I pleaded.

'Soon, sir, soon ...'

The light, the radiance faded just as quickly as it had appeared. I was once again alone.

Michael, Age 17
Outback NSW, Australia, 1998

Those next summer holidays proved to be more of a revelation than most others. A turning point, call it what you like. The reality was that I was beginning to feel the presence of a man within the body of the boy. I guess a caterpillar feels the same way when it exits its cocoon as a butterfly. Anyway, enough of the descriptive analogies; whatever the turning point was, it felt like a heady mix of testosterone, risk analysis, capacity building and good fortune.

Mum and I were pretty cool; we always were. She was still going flat out trying to keep our tiny household afloat. I guess she had lost the notion that a boy needed a father and, despite the odd date she went out on, she didn't bring anybody home in an effort to be my next 'father'. That was all fine by me. I was happy in my own developing body and unfolding world. After all, unlike many of the guys I knew at school, I wasn't any problem for my mother. I didn't rebel; I was neither rude nor morose, and I was far from argumentative. In fact, I considered myself pretty lucky, really. I even tried my best to put some food on the table when I could. I think Mum really appreciated the help. But most of all, I knew the time had come. It was time for live practice.

The routine was pretty simple. After breakfast, when Mum would drive out to her next shift, I would help around the kitchen and clean up the morning's dishes. Mum always smiled at me as she left for work. That was cool because I was able to stuff my backpack full of a day's provisions. Everything I would need for the probabilities of the day. I mean, I didn't have to lug much, just enough for a light lunch and enough water just in case I couldn't find any. Once equipped, I was out to the shed to collect my prized arsenal.

I didn't know how I knew. Maybe it was all of the reading I had done, but somehow I just understood how to transport my rifle. Maybe it was through osmosis from a previous generation, but I just knew how to handle the weapon with safety. I knew it as a means of destruction and was sensible enough to treat it with respect. I wasn't scared, or anything, it's just that I was aware of its dark side – the wicked power of the combined man/boy and machine.

I carried the gun at shoulder-arms just like I had seen in books and on television. There was never a bullet in the breech, and the safety was always on. When walking uphill or down dale, I was particularly cautious when crouching through the odd barbed wire fence. I knew the gun was only lethal when all of its component parts were framed to a specific purpose – like when it was loaded and the safety was off. Despite all of my risk aversion, I tripped once and fell flat on my face – I shit myself, but no damage was done.

The morning I had chosen to start hunting was more than I could have wished for. The sun had risen above the horizon with barely a cloud in the sky. Even the gentle breeze was kind enough to keep the sweat at bay from lugging my pack and gun. It felt somehow magical to be out bush on my own. It felt as if I were one with nature. As if the world of cities and towns and people were a whole other world away. I sensed the breeze and could gauge its strength and direction. Air temperature made a difference, too.

When I first spotted a target, it was as if I could do the calculations in my head. Distance a hundred metres, wind speed southerly at ten knots. I didn't need a computer – I had one in my head. Mind you, in the early days, I did miss more than I hit. I started with large objects first. Tree stumps and old cans were favourites. Funnily enough, the more I practised the better I got. By the third day of aiming at and mostly hitting inanimate objects, I knew I was ready to graduate to real things. But my first 'kill' would always remain my weirdest.

I had the mid-morning sun at my back and the slight breeze was barely ruffling the tumbleweeds, so my human scent wasn't a factor. But the heat was already making a shimmering haze across the expanse of the scorched terrain. I had taken up a position on a slight elevation, under a really large ghost-gum, about two hundred metres from a small watering hole.

I knew if I was patient enough, something would come along, and it did. It always did. I was patient enough. I'd made a soft bed of dried leaves and underbrush, just enough to remove the slight discomfort of lying prone in wait.

I didn't mind the waiting. In fact, it was kind of fun. It allowed my mind to wander off on its own. Not lose the awareness of my purpose, mind. I was still focused through the aperture. My mind was alive to the prospect of something appearing in the crosshairs. It was just that another part of my conscious mind was free to roam through a variety of past memories. There were all of these rooms I could enter. Music was a favourite. I heard it. Sometimes it was the beat of the latest top-40 hit, but sometimes it sounded like a choral choir. It was beautiful, but I only heard it sometimes. It seemed to just turn up when it felt like it. Anyway, I wasn't complaining.

Sure enough, a small marsupial appeared in the crosshairs – a rock wallaby. I didn't hesitate; I didn't think. I squeezed softly on the trigger, just like I had taught myself to do. I didn't miss. That wasn't the issue at all. I was getting pretty good at hitting things, but what I saw was really weird.

I didn't know whether it was the shimmering effect of the mid-morning sun or a vague trick of vision distorted by the small pond of water in the background. I saw the wallaby leap in the air as the bullet struck mid-section and without warning. The small body gave a couple of twitches before its lights went out. That's when it got really weird. I was still looking through the aperture when I saw what I think I saw but couldn't explain. It was as if the spirit of the wallaby arose from its dead form. The wallaby's spirit floated momentarily over its now lifeless body. Then, as if it were liberated from its harsher confines, it floated off into the air. I lost sight of it after that, but that memory of my first real 'kill' never left me.

Anyway, Mum was pretty happy. I made up a story about how a mate and I had gone out bush, and he'd shot a couple of critters and shared one with me. Mum smiled at me and suggested that we might be able to sell some at the local abattoir to earn an extra dollar or two. I told her I'd check it out and mention it to my mate next time we went out. She was happy with that.

I must say that Mum was pretty dexterous with a knife, too. She had the critter gutted and skinned in no time at all.

CHAPTER 10

Matthew J. Cooper
Heaven

It wasn't like I had time on my hands or anything, it was just that I guessed I might have finished with the kaleidoscope thing, but I wasn't sure. I was reclining under the largest and most majestic ghost-gum tree I had ever seen. The tree sat upon a small hill surrounded by an expanse of green pasturage swaying in a gentle breeze. It was beautiful. It reminded me of parts of the outback when I was 'alive' – but this place was even more alive.

I couldn't even begin to describe the colours. If you could image the seven colours of the rainbow magnified by a factor ten, you might begin to get the picture. One part of me was revelling in the moving expanse of colours and light while another part of 'me' was pondering my experience with Jonathan. His final words kept resonating through my being, 'Soon, sir, soon.' It was all kind of hard to fathom because here, wherever 'here' was, I had no sense of time. 'Soon' didn't have any link to my current sense of reality.

Anyway, no matter, I thought. Things seemed to happen 'here' whether you liked them or not. There didn't seem to be any procrastination, 'elephant in the room' or 'hide and go seek' about it. Things happened whether you wanted them to or not.

Mind you, that immediate thought did have consequences because my kaleidoscope suddenly appeared and started to go AWOL. I felt the heat even before I sensed the presence. The vivid red and burning heat was like no other that I had ever seen or felt before. It was like a thousand infernos all focused from a single point. I reached up and touched that part of the kaleidoscope; I just couldn't resist.

'God help me!' I said out loud in response to wherever I was, and, 'Holy hell,' to the heat. It felt hotter than a blast furnace. It wasn't so much a wall of fire as a wall of heat, and it seemed to emanate from a single source. There was a focal point. I tried my best to stay calm in the face of this avalanche, but it was overwhelming. I closed my eyes and tried to find my centre, the place I always went to when I was waiting. That kind of worked. At least it gave me a sense of balance in the face of the torrent. It enabled me to find some words, albeit terrified ones.

'Who are you? What do you want with me?' I mumbled.

To whatever it was, this question was like a red flag to a bull. The heat only became stronger. Then I saw it. At least I began to see its outline through the haze of heat and anger. Yes, that's what it was. I recognised it now. It wasn't heat from fire ... It was heat from anger. *Holy smoke*, I thought, *whoever, or whatever it is, sure is pissed at something.*

I managed to stammer in the face of the onslaught. 'Who are you? What do you want with me? What have I done to make you so angry?'

The words had their desired effect. He burst into my vision like a charging bull. I could see his form clearly, but the heat from his anger shimmered like a thousand suns. He was surrounded by a shimmering poisonous red haze and thermal heat poured from his eyes like a demon.

'Do you not remember me, vermin?'

I tried my best to peer through the heat haze but failed in an effort to recognise my antagonist.

'Sorry,' I said trying to be as calm as I could. 'I just don't know who you are.'

That really did set the cat amongst the pigeons. Great flames of anger erupted from his being like bolts of lightning.

'Witless vermin! Scum! Parasite!' he hollered. 'You are the one who killed me.'

'I am?' I said as amiably as I could in the face of his wrath while I hastily sped through my memories to pinpoint the exact recollection of the incident in question. After all, I had killed a lot of people, enemy mostly.

'Look,' I said as forthrightly as I could. 'I killed a lot of people. It was war! I killed the enemy, as many as I could, in fact. If you were one, well then, I'm sorry, fella, that's just the way it goes. I got you before you got me, okay!'

Now that really pissed him off because bolts of red-hot beams sparked like a hot iron on an anvil. It was as if he were trying to engulf me in his anger, but I stayed as calm as I could. After all, I had to figure out what was going on. Why I was here.

'Like I said, I'm sorry I killed you, but what's with all the anger? It was war after all.'

His eyes flared like hot embers as they bore into my own.

'You are nothing but scum, you and your kind. It was you that caused the subjugation of our people. You that set all of the evil upon our fatherland! It was you who placed our people beneath the heel of your decrepit Empire. You had to be killed, all of you. You had to be exterminated – you were all vermin, you and your race, all of your kind.'

It was lucky I was calm because at one level of my awareness I was saying to myself, 'Thank God, I killed this piece of shit.' Listening to his incoherent rant about the war was almost too much to bear. But, there was another part of me that tried to understand the depths of my current predicament. I was in a deep pile of poop, that was for sure.

'Look, fella, I don't know who you think you are, but I wasn't any vermin, do you understand? I was just a regular guy serving my nation. After all, you and your so-called 'master-race' wanted to take over the world. Now that just wasn't going to happen as far as I was concerned. You and your kind set the world to fire, not me. I was just trying to put the fire out.'

I saw his chest heave and sparks of anger erupt from the apex of his head ... But then I got an idea.

'Look, tell me something ... what caused you to think that we were all vermin, all scum that had to be exterminated? I mean, couldn't you see that we were humans, too? Geez, after all, we were all flesh and blood. All of us felt pain and suffering. We all bled when struck. The pain and suffering you caused millions upon millions of people has flowed through a multitude of generations. Why? Why did you do it?'

Again, bolts of lightning-sparked from his being, but there was something else. I couldn't quite put my finger on it, but I thought I saw the intensity of the red-colour abate. Like it had been mixed with another colour, blue, perhaps.

'You were all scum,' he repeated.

'Yeah, I know, you told me that, and I don't buy it. I mean, where did you learn such crap? Who taught you such nonsense?'

I watched carefully to see his reaction and at least saw a crinkle as his eyebrows drew together, so I got a bit more game and reached out my hand to touch his red-hot energy. Immediately, I was transported through his memory banks. I saw him as a child, dressed in his quaint little Aryan uniform and being indoctrinated day-after-day into the isms of the 'master-race'. I saw him spat upon and subjugated for doing something wrong and beaten when he would not follow orders. I saw the innocence of his childhood forged into a distorted semblance of a human being.

All of these images passed through me in an instant, and I withdrew my hand as if it had been scolded in a burning cauldron. But at least I had begun to understand the nature of the being before me.

I wasn't sure where it came from, but I did my best to express what next came to mind.

'Like I said, I'm sorry I killed you. I can understand your anger, but maybe it's best we try this another way.'

I watched carefully as his eyebrows knitted together, again.

'What are you talking about?' he replied.

Streuth, I thought, *that's a win. At least he's stopped calling me 'vermin'.*

'I understand your anger, but it seems to me that hanging on to all of that stuff is not doing you any good. I mean, look at you! There has to be another way of looking at it.'

'Huh?' was his reply as I watched a blue colour mix with the red.

I'm not sure where the next words came from. They didn't sound like me, but I went with them anyway. 'Well, perhaps, anger and violence are not the same things.'

'What are you talking about?' he said with a hint more circumspection.

'Well, anger is natural, isn't it? It's okay to feel angry. It seems to me to be perfectly natural. It's like when I was doing my job; I was a sniper after all. I was never angry. It never served me to be angry. I was always calm.'

'Yes, well, all that may be so, but ...'

'But, nothing,' I butted in rather rudely. *This was getting kind of interesting*, I thought at one level of my consciousness as a flash of memory whizzed past of my own unopened door to 'that' room from the centre of my being.

'Wouldn't it be better to release your anger in some other way? I mean, perhaps all this anger that you feel about me and my kind could be released in a better way. Not through violence or retribution, but through, but through ...' as I struggled for the right word. 'Wonder! Yes, wonder.'

'Wonder! Have you lost your mind?' he roared, with sparks of filament red shooting out from him.

Maybe, I thought, *he might be right; I had lost my mind.* But then a revelation dawned. The answer came without bidding. It was just there.

'Wouldn't it be wonderful if you could release your anger in wonder, I mean. Then you could be at peace and not have to suffer like you are.'

I watched carefully as his twisted thoughts jostled across his red visage with the notion of my proposal. 'But, how ...?' he asked.

'I wonder if you can conceive of a time when children are shown that violence is not the way to solve problems. I wonder if they can be taught to solve problems with love ... Rather than hate. How good would that be, huh?'

I saw a deep blue colour enter the outer reaches of his energy field. Mind you, it wasn't as if it was totally overwhelming. It was just that it seemed to cool the embers of his rage. It brought cooling water where only before fire had raged. *Maybe it was enough*, I thought, *just enough.*

In the background, just to the outer reach of my senses, I heard music. It was beautiful. It was calling me.

'Look, it was nice meeting you, but I have to go,' I said as I raised my hand in farewell. He didn't smile as I watched him fade into the background, but I saw the colour blue shoot from his energy field as I closed the door behind me. I couldn't help my deep exhale of breath as I heard the door click shut behind me.

Then, out of nowhere, Jonathan appeared right in front of me. I saw him smile at me. But then, all of an instant, his face changed ... it changed to Michael's face ... my beloved grandson, Michael.

'I told you it would be soon, didn't I, sir?' he said.

I almost dropped my bundle.

CHAPTER 11

Michael, Age 17
Outback NSW, Australia, 1998

I guess the universe had its way of drawing two kindred spirits together. Stuff happened that ensured kindred paths crossed. I mean, I knew Mum and I were both kin and kindred. I didn't have to be Einstein to figure that one out. The problem was, Mum was my only point of reference. Yeah, sure, as a teenager I'd looked at a bit of porn, but I sure as hell knew that wasn't any sort of answer. I remember sneaking glances at some pretty girls when I was at school. I even recall working up the courage to ask one of them out on a date. The fact that she said 'no' didn't bother me overly.

I asked Mum once about girls and stuff. All she said with a smile was that, 'When the time is right, these things just happen. When you are ready, the stars align and lives intersect.'

She was pretty wise, my mum, because that's pretty much what happened, and it happened when I wasn't even looking for it to happen. I wasn't complaining because even though I knew her, I hadn't really met her before. Well, whatever the case, it was good. It was more than a young man thought he deserved, that's for sure.

Given that Mum was pretty happy for me to contribute to the wellbeing of our little household as much as possible, I was determined to pursue the possibilities with the local abattoir. My next kill, a medium-sized kangaroo, was offered up in exchange for a few dollars. The bloody thing was heavy. I had to lug it more kilometres than I cared to remember. Not to mention that I had to construct a well-concealed hiding spot for my arsenal before entering the industrial premises.

I was only a few months further on from my seventeenth birthday, and I had no expectation of being wise or experienced in the complex ways of human attraction. Yet, as soon as I opened the door to the administration area of the abattoir, I knew something was going on. I could only see her face and a small portion of the rest of her torso above the counter. Maybe it was the blast from the chilled air-conditioning, but I think not. I gave an involuntary shudder when I looked into her eyes. I remembered my manners, too. After all, I had been brought up right by Mum. I removed my cap and brushed dirt from the front of my rather scruffy jacket, then wiped my dirty boots on the mat provided – but it was if I were mesmerised, rooted to the spot. I couldn't move until she expressed a welcome smile and asked if she could help me.

My tentative movement forwards, clutching my cap, gave me some moments to search for a calm centre that I couldn't find, but her smile helped.

'You're Michael, aren't you? From our school?' she asked, and her voice gave me goose bumps.

'Ah, yeah, um, yes!' I managed to mumble in reply.

'You're in the class next to mine, aren't you? Year 11, Class A. I'm in Class B.'

I managed a smile when I realised who she was. I had seen her before, many times, but hadn't recognised her. I guess it was the fact that she was not in school uniform. Maybe it was because she was now in this different environment. Perhaps it was the slight coverage of rouge on her cheeks that girls weren't allowed to wear at school. Whatever the case, my brain didn't register instant recognition, but I felt something, that was for sure.

'Hi, my name is Angela, but people call me Angel ...' she said as she stood up from her chair and offered me her hand across the great divide of the customer counter. She was dressed in a pretty free-flowing floral dress that seemed to brighten the green colour of her eyes. The dress made her look like she was surrounded by a flower garden.

Her hand felt like the touch of silk on my dirt-encrusted mitt. I almost gasped for breath, my nerves threatening to overwhelm my brain of how to speak properly and behave nicely in front of women. I recovered just in the nick of time.

I felt an instant attraction. I wasn't exactly sure what love was, but this sure felt like a connection to it. I mean, I'd touched girls before, and I'd hugged Mum plenty of times, but that didn't count, she wasn't a girl, was she. 'I was just wondering how much I could get for the kangaroo I brought in?' I said as I thumbed in the direction outside the doorway.

'No problem,' she answered with a knowing smile. 'Just go back into the shed and ask for Frank. He's the foreman. Show him what you've got, and he'll let me know how much it's worth. Then come back in and I'll give you the money, okay?'

I mumbled my thanks in understanding of the process and turned to retrace my unwilling steps back into the shed. My meeting with Frank the foreman was much easier. He was a bloke.

I returned to the blast of cool air-conditioning. She had the exact monies waiting for me on the counter.

'Thanks,' I mumbled as I picked up the notes and loose change and asked if I could do this again.

'Sure,' she said, 'come by whenever you like. I'll be here. At least during school holidays, I will be.'

I looked at her cheeks, pinched red from the chill of the air-conditioning. 'Does that you mean you'll be going back to school next year?' I asked.

'Yeah, of course,' she replied as she looked around furtively. 'I won't be working in an abattoir all my life, that's for sure.' I nodded in mutual understanding. 'What about you? Are you going back?'

'Yeah, I suppose so. Nothing else to do. At least not yet,' I replied.

'I guess I'll see you 'round, then,' I added. 'Next time I come in, that is.'

I wasn't sure, but I think I saw a hint of a spark behind her eyes as a smile lit up her face.

'Yeah, see you next time. That'll be good,' Angela added.

It was funny because as I walked back to where I'd secreted my M40, it seemed as if I were walking on air. I couldn't quite work out why, but I guessed it was because I had my head stuck inside the number nine cloud. I couldn't wait to plot the time of my next excursion and had 'ants in my pants' for my next 'kill'.

Matthew J. Cooper
Heaven

I wasn't in the place where I belonged for very long. It almost felt as if all of this 'important 'life review' stuff' was happening at once. In fact, this business of time, or 'no time', whatever it was, was really messing with my 'head'. I couldn't figure it out. I looked down to see that a silver cord, one going straight to my heart, was activated. The colour was vibrant and vibrating. It looked like Michael's cord, but I knew it was different. I couldn't resist as I reached down into it, just like I'd done before. I felt the love instantly, but couldn't understand why I hadn't seen this cord before.

She was waiting for me. It was like meeting her for the first time. I felt the same instant attraction, the same connection – to love.

The magnificence and majesty of the flowers and abundant flora that surrounded her almost overshadowed the excitement of being with her again. She was surrounded within the radiance of an ornate garden. The free-flowing floral robe she wore seemed to help her blend into the garden around her. The multi-play of colours was like none that I had ever seen. It was as if her heart had bloomed and given birth to regal pageantry. She was a part of nature and nature was a part of her. This was the woman I had loved ... and still did.

When she spoke, it felt as if my heart was fit to explode.

'Hello,' was all she said, as her smile of love said more than words ever could. 'I've been waiting for you.'

I tried my best to stop my heart from bursting, but failed miserably. If this was happiness, then it had surely been in short supply when she wasn't there – by my side.

Our embrace was worth more than life itself, and at one level I wondered how I'd ever managed without it.

'We do have things to talk about, you and I, don't we?' she said in confirmation of the obvious.

'Margaret, I, I ...' I stammered not able to make sense of the tumbledown of thoughts and emotions coursing through my being.

'Yes, my love, my husband, I know that you don't understand ... but you will, in time. Soon, you will, soon.'

Funny, I thought, *that's exactly what Jonathan had said. I wonder how that works?*

Her face crinkled in a knowing smile as she placed a gentle hand to my cheek. It felt like the touch of an angel.

'I'm sorry,' I said, feeling the heavy weight of lost time. 'I would have been here sooner, but I don't know how things work in this place. I mean, I'm not even sure where I am.'

She tilted her head to one side, just enough to indicate that she understood. 'There is no need to be sorry. There is nothing to be sorry for. There is no time and space here ... just an eternal 'now'.'

I kind of understood what she was talking about, but then she added, 'You could not have come even if you had wanted to. You had to experience the consequences of your life before you could be with me.'

I didn't say anything, but my perplexed look said enough.

'Our love is our bond. It will always be there, forever. That's what the silver cord is, silly,' she added with a cheeky grin. 'Just like with Michael.'

'You know about Michael?' I asked hesitantly.

'Of course. We are all kin. Love knows no bounds in such regard.'

In an instant, I was overwhelmed. A spate of memory and repressed emotion came flooding back over me. She had to reach for me to hold me from crumpling to the ground.

'I was so lost after you passed. After you died, I mean. I missed you so much. You were the one thing in my life that made any sense.' A flood of more bottled-up emotion followed as my chest heaved in an effort to sustain itself. 'Why did you have to die? Why did cancer take you and leave me? It should have been me. I was the one who killed. I am the one who should be punished. You, you were like a beautiful flower. You didn't deserve all of that pain. All of that suffering! I couldn't help you! I couldn't do anything! I would have changed places in an instant if I could have.'

'Yes, my love, I know. That is the beauty of your heart. That is why our love will forever be,' she said with the reassurance of a smile and a gentle touch to my cheek.

I pushed away any lingering regret then went searching for her hand.

'Can we go now? I mean, can we be together?'

She looked down at the silver cord between us, vivid and vibrating with a colour brighter than the sun. 'We always were. Always will be. But here, where we are, there are many mansions. First, you must hear the music. Listen for the music; that is where I will be.'

As she spoke, her head cocked slightly to the right. 'I hear it now; they are calling me,' she said as she began to fade into the beauty of the floral background. It was as if she became one with everything that ever was and ever is.

'Who? Who is calling you? I don't understand.'

'Soon, my love, soon, you will hear the music,' were her words that echoed through the ethers and pierced my soul – again.

CHAPTER 12

Michael, Age 17
Outback NSW, Australia, 1998

It wasn't as if I was any kind of Don Juan or anything. I mean, I didn't wear fancy clothes or come from some rich, privileged background of entitlement. I wasn't even a member of the local football team. I didn't have big muscles or a big brain. I was just a regular dude, working class, no more or no less than anybody else. The fact of the matter was, though, I knew what I liked and I knew what my inner-senses were telling me. It wasn't a testosterone-fuelled impulse either, that's for sure. Nor did I have any idea what love was, but I was fairly certain I was pretty close. Even so, it took me three more visits with three more 'kills' to work up the courage to ask if Angela would like to go out for lunch or something.

I've had some disappointments before. I knew what rejection was. None of which bothered me over-much. But the thought of her saying no to my fumble-tongued advances was enough to fill me with dread. I thanked all of my lucky stars after she said she'd meet me after work next Saturday, and that we could go to the local café for a bite. Fortunately, she gave me some sound advice and recommended I wear a nicer jacket. I looked down at my filthy jacket with a notion of understanding.

The Friday evening before the big event, Mum even mentioned that my haircut looked good. I think she might have twigged that I was meeting a girl, but didn't press the issue, leaving open the option to talk to her about 'girl things' if I ever felt the need. I managed to mumble my thanks for the nice dinner before shuffling off to my room to nervously count the minutes till dawn breaking a new beginning.

I still didn't know how these things happened and I certainly didn't know why, but as I planted my behind on the side of the bed, I had this really strong urge to read Grandpa's diary again. It would take my mind off other things, I reasoned as I reached under the bed for the leather satchel. As I opened the leather binds and held the diary in my hands for a few moments, I swore I could see my grandfather sitting in his recliner chair speaking to me. I couldn't quite make out what he was saying, but I was sure he was smiling as he reached down to touch something near his heart.

Quite unexpectedly, as soon I opened the diary, a small photograph fell onto my lap. I picked it up and looked at the grainy-coloured image. It was a photograph of a young woman. She was very pretty in a wholesome kind of way. Her long blonde hair cascaded over her shoulders, and her eyes sparkled with a sense of radiated happiness, despite the grainy image. If I were to take a guess, it looked as if she was about eighteen or nineteen years old. She was standing amidst a beautiful garden full of plants and wildflowers. It was as if she were a part of nature. As if she were one with the plants and flowers. They loved her and she loved them. I'd never seen anything like it – it was weird. I stared at the photo for I don't know how long before my eyes were drawn back to the diary entry from which the photo had fallen loose. It was a handwritten note. It looked like my grandpa's scrawl – hard to decipher, but readable none-the-less:

Received a letter from Margaret today along with this old photo. I remember taking it. It was the day before I was to leave for the war. It brought back a lot of memories. She is so beautiful. I remember we made love on a soft bed of flowers that same afternoon and almost got caught by the local gardener. How she laughed when I tripped over myself pulling my strides up.

I miss the girl, that's for sure. I mean, if I get out of this hell-hole alive, I'll make sure I never leave her side. For the life of me, I've never understood what she sees in me. I'm a killer, after all. That's what I do. I kill people, and she's as sweet as a shower of rain on a wasteland.

I guess it's best if I just keep the photo here in the diary, and I'll try to keep her out of my mind. Best not to get distracted, I reckon, as it might make my hands shake. I might miss.

Anyway, when (if) I get back from this mission tomorrow, I promise I'll write her a letter. It's the least I can do. Geez, I hope she waits for me. If I get out of here, I hope I'll be the same man she fell in love with. Don't know about that, really. The nightmares are getting stronger. I can't sleep. Sometimes I wake up frightened, too. I see their faces … they're all waiting for me, every one of them.

The entry was finished with a hasty signature. I wonder what Grandpa meant by 'they're all waiting for me, every one of them'? That really didn't make much sense. Anyway, I looked at the photo once again then flipped it over to see what was written on the back. This was in a different, more floral, handwriting and said:

Our love is our bond. It will always be there, forever.

It was signed, Margaret. She must have been the grandmother I never knew. Mum had told me she'd died before I was born.

I closed the diary and re-tied the leather thong, but kept the picture safely to hand. It was pinned securely on the wall next to the other two photos of Grandpa.

Matthew J. Cooper
Heaven

I wasn't sure how long I stayed in that space after Margaret left. Given my current mixed-up notions about time in this place, I wasn't even sure if it was more than a few moments, but it sure felt like it. I didn't know whether to laugh or cry. Having again seen Margaret, the love of my life, to know that she was alright, filled my heart with pure joy. On the other hand, I felt destitute. The fact that I could not be with her, made me feel as if I were an exiled lost soul cast aside on the rocky shores of a remote isle. The question, 'What do I have to do?' kept repeating itself through my mind. As I recall it, I even yelled into the ethers in hope that someone was listening. Given the events that soon unfolded, I guess someone was.

My 'life review' thing felt like it was going completely off the charts. The vivid scarlet colour and the feeling of discomfort emanating from my kaleidoscope felt as irresistible as it was undeniable. My hand was drawn to the colour like a moth to a flame. I could not resist – but maybe I should have ...

Immediately, my experience of pain went through the roof. It were as if I'd been cut in two, or had a piece of my internals ripped from me by rough, uncaring hands. The sensation was so acute, I could neither see nor relate to anything around me. It was like I had been cast into a dense fog – and there was only agony. I could neither discern nor care what was around me. I cried out to all or any of the Gods to make the hurt stop, and I guess someone listened. The anguish immediately ceased and the fog lifted. Only my gasping breath and hands clasped to knees betrayed that I had experienced anything at all. That is, until my vision cleared. That's when I saw him.

The man/being that stood before me was a replica of some-one I had seen through the aperture of my scope, but I know I wasn't much good at remembering faces. It was always the uni-form I tried to focus on. But I guess it was something like a car crash, wasn't it. You saw the car but there was always some-body behind the wheel. There was always a human being buried under the insignia on the uniform.

He was about my height, but a bit younger. What differenti-ated us, however, was the livid scar down the left side of his face. He'd been cut from chin to earlobe with an extended part of his ear and cheek sown together as if to keep the rest of his face from falling out. He was a mess. He looked at me with eyes that pierced the depths of my soul.

'You don't remember me, do you?' he asked in a rather slurred sort of way as if his tongue didn't quite function within the confines of its rearranged home.

I did my best to sift and strain through the corridors of my mind, but it didn't work. I couldn't pin the memory down.

'Look, sorry, I don't remember,' was all I could manage in response.

He reached up with his left hand to gently touch the remains of the left side of his mangled visage.

'You did this. Do you remember now?'

Again, my lost voice and perplexed look was enough to give him the response he sought.

'You missed!' he said emphatically. 'At least, I didn't die straight away. I lived for another six months ... with the pain.'

'But, but, I never missed. I always killed,' I mumbled, horrified. 'I never let them suffer. I always aimed for the heart. I didn't want any one of them to suffer, don't you understand?'

'You missed!' was all he said in repetition as another wave of experiential hurt pierced my body like a bolt of sheer lightning.

'Aarghh, stop it! Whatever it is that you are doing, please, stop it,' I shouted into his mind with a grimace. Immediately the anguish ceased, and I was able to relax.

'What is that? How are you doing that?' I said as soon as I was able.

'Me? I do nothing,' he replied.

'Then, what? How?' I replied.

He looked at me in some kind of understanding and perhaps a hint of empathy.

'That is what I experienced, all of that physical pain ... and emotional anguish.'

'Huh? I don't understand?'

'You missed my heart, but your bullet blew away the left side of my face,' he said as he again touched his dilapidated jaw line. 'I survived.'

I could only stand, mute, open-mouthed in the face of the consequences of my actions.

'I'm sorry,' was all I could stammer after I found part of my voice. 'I didn't know; I didn't mean to. I never wanted it, any of it. I always shot to kill. Never to maim.'

He looked at me with eyes that held a depth of understanding mixed with retribution.

'But why, why am I feeling all of this anguish? This hurt? I don't understand.'

'You are experiencing what I experienced as a result of what you did. That is what it is – consequences.'

'Is this retribution for what I did? You are punishing me for what I did to you, aren't you?' I said with what I thought was the birth of understanding.

Again, he looked at me with that look somewhere between understanding, empathy and malice.

'No,' he replied stoically, 'this could not be further from the truth. 'Where we are, there is no such thing as "reward and punishment". There is only evolution. You are simply evolving.'

'Evolving! You call this evolving? What the f**k are you talking about?' I shouted as I sensed another bolt of hurt approach through the ethers.

'The purpose of this experience, your evolution, is to show you your humanity to yourself. To show that what you to do another is the same as you do to yourself. "What you sow, so shall you reap" is the law that you have now experienced ... even if you "didn't know".'

'Oh, my God! I am so sorry,' I said again.

'Do not be sorry. There is no need. Don't you see? I am here, and I am loved beyond my wildest expectations – just like you are.' He said these words with as much of a smile as his broken face would allow. Then he began to fade into the background. He seemed to just meld into the fold of cloud and mist. As I watched him fade, I noticed that what was before a vivid colour of purple in the field of energy that surrounded him had been replaced by a more intense blue colour. I wasn't much for colour therapy, but I figured that blue was the colour of healing.

I guess we have both been healed by this experience, I mused.

The instant this thought appeared, I heard an answer that was as clear as the dawning sunshine.

'Yes! Yes, you have! You both have!' said the voice. 'And this is why you must help Michael.'

CHAPTER 13

Michael, Age 17
Outback NSW, Australia, 1998

Man! I'd never been so nervous in all of my life. My palms were sweating, and I was pacing up and down as if I had ants in my pants. I kept on glancing at the sidewalk clock just outside the café and I swear the hands never moved once. Even when they did and reached the appointed hour, they moved even slower. *Thank God, I'm not trying to shoot my rifle*, I thought. *I wouldn't be able to hit the side of a barn.*

I was put out of my misery when Angela arrived with a smile and the scent of fresh flowers in the air. To me, she looked like a goddess in her floral dress, with her golden hair that fell over her shoulders. As the midday sun caught her from behind, it made it seem like she had a golden glow that would do justice to an angel. I couldn't help but stare.

'What are you looking at?' she said with feigned mockery.

'I'm sorry,' I mumbled as she smiled at my discomfort, but that all vanished when she took my hand and directed me into the café.

'Let's go eat,' she said with a bounce, 'I'm starving.'

It was not the most wholesome of eating establishments, but to me, it seemed as if we were not far removed from seventh heaven. The menu wasn't much to write home about, either, but I couldn't have cared less. I was sitting with an angel.

It wasn't so much that I was overcome by any sense of teenage-riddled, testosterone-filled desire to land my first conquest. My thoughts were centred well above my navel. It was more like I was suddenly surrounded by an unknown world of love and all its mysteries. I'm not even sure what we ate. I remember putting food in my mouth, but not how it tasted. I was too focused on watching her every little move – how her dimples deepened when she smiled, how her eyes shone when she was speaking about her family and her love of nature. I listened to her every word, and every syllable felt like a soft touch to my ears. The best part was when she told me that I even 'scrubbed-up all right' given my recently cut hair, clean fingernails and polished sneakers.

I learned a lot about Angela that day. I learned of her desire to become a botanist. I learned of her attachment to family and the power of her social convictions. The whole scene was a portrait of a beautiful heart. I was pretty sure that if I could ever paint a masterpiece, she would be my Mona Lisa. She was an open book. Disclosure of her inner feelings and dreams came easy. Me, on the other hand, I was like a tin can of unopened mysteries, but, once opened, my words soon became a torrent. I couldn't stop.

I told her all about my beautiful mum. I even told her about 'the bastard' stepfather. I told her all about my 'killing' expeditions and how I was helping Mum put food on the table and pennies in the jar. That made her smile. She neither judged nor condemned my 'killing' of animals for the higher cause of familial support. She wasn't even worried about me hurting myself or doing bad things with a powerful weapon. She seemed to know that I was a well-balanced human being and that my heart was firmly fixed to the correct side of the ledger. She was pretty chuffed, too, when I told her that I only ever shot to kill, never to suffer. I was too good a shot. I never missed and always aimed for the heart. That bit made her kind of wince and smile at the same time.

When I finally looked up and away from her eyes, the clock on the sidewall had run away with itself. Hours had flown, and it was time to go. She was due back home to help her mum with the evening meal. The best part was the plans we made to meet and go to the movies at the same time next weekend. I also promised to bring in another 'kill' during the last week before we had to go back to school for the new scholastic year. *School was never going to be the same again*, I mused as I rather clumsily held out my hand for her to shake. But she ignored that and gave me a lingering hug. It was a hug that will never be forgotten.

Mum noticed my distraction over the dinner table that night, but she was content with a knowing smile of understanding to leave me to my reveries. She even gave me a leave-pass from the dishes. Given such, I hastened to my bedroom where the best I could do was just stare at the ceiling and day-dream about things I didn't know much about. I even tried reading Grandpa's diary for some insight into this new roman-tic world order, but I was too distracted. I couldn't concentrate.

Matthew J. Cooper
Heaven

I was hopeful of a brief interlude, some rest after my recent experience with the disfigured man. I had to try and make sense of everything. 'This is why you must help Michael,' the voice had said. Help him? I thought I had. I mean, whatever I had to do, I would. I loved him. But what about me? What about the music? Why couldn't I hear my music? All I wanted was a little time where I could figure some of this out. But, alas, it was not to be. I looked down at my chest and saw one of my silver cords blazing like the midday sun. I knew it was Michael's; I recognised the colour and the feeling. I knew he was okay, but I didn't know how. All I knew was that a lightning bolt of Marga-ret's sweet face flashed through my being and carried with it a scent of the familiar and comfortable. Then I heard her sweet voice through the ethers.

'Patience, my love, everything will be revealed. Michael's love for another has to be born ... just like ours was. This will be his saviour ... just like our love was for you ... and me.'

I couldn't help but smile, and leaned back against the large ghost-gum tree that had become my favourite refuge in this place. But no sooner had I closed my eyes and exhaled a deep sigh, something else happened. Something I hadn't seen before and certainly did not recognise burst open before me. There was most assuredly the colour purple, but it was intertwined with a rich, dark pink. I didn't know what it was about these colours, they were so much more intense and descriptive in this place to what I had previously known. But the kaleidoscope again proved irresistible to the touch and transported me in an instant to where I needed to be ...

Mud and slush were everywhere. The heavy smell of cordite filled the air with an overwhelming omen of doom. I remembered the scene vividly and could still feel the rumble of the heavy artillery as it thankfully moved westward from our current position. The bombardment had moved on, but the consequential trail of destruction remained in its wake.

I'd made my kill. I'd done my job, and I'd done it right. Target dispatched, sine-missione, no mercy shown, none given. I was making my way back through the wooded destruction of war to the security of life behind the lines when I heard the cry. It was a sound like the hoot of an owl, but then again, it wasn't. Even owls were averse to flight in this wasteland of death and destitution. My instincts of self-preservation instantly activated as I moved the M40 smoothly from my shoulder and primed the breech in readiness for impulsive action. My ears twitched in search of danger and my eyes

narrowed to peer through the gloom and smoke like a submariners'
periscope in search of prey. Then clarity came. I didn't understand
the words, but I understood the meaning well enough.

'Hilf mir, bitte.'

I followed the sound waves to a bomb crater amidst a ramshack-
le mix of twisted metal, broken timber and concrete rubble. With
every sense twitching, I raised myself just high enough to peer over
the edge.

'Hilf mir, aagh,' came the words filled with agony.

I was able to see enough and deemed that I was not in any im-
minent danger so disengaged the bolt of my M40, replaced the strap
to my shoulder and removed my Colt in anticipation of probable
use.

The soldier's right leg had been blown completely off. God only
knew what else was wrong with him. His camouflage uniform was
a tattered mess of shrapnel holes and encrusted mud and grime. I
felt the tension in my shoulders ease as I saw his rifle was just out-
side the limit of his extended reach. It was a Mauser 98. I knew this
to be the favourite of his kind. He was a sniper, an enemy sniper,
just like me. But he wore the wrong uniform. He was my enemy, not
my comrade. I took in the mangled condition of his surrounds and
figured that he must have been holed-up in the building and had
been taking aim at our troops some 700 metres to the east, given the
slightly elevated position of the territory. The bastard was killing
our boys, I thought as my finger twitched on the trigger of the Colt.
I approached him through the blood and mud.

I deliberately cleared my mind of any sense of lingering doubt as
I cocked the Colt and placed the barrel against his exposed temple. It
would be a mercy, I thought. Besides, he was the enemy. He'd been

killing our boys. The son of a bitch deserved what he was going to
get, didn't he? This was sine-missione, no quarter given, none asked
for. Kill or be killed, that's all there was. Right? That was until I
looked into his eyes. I wasn't sure what I saw. I guess it was like
looking into a mirror. Deep below all of his anguish and pain, I
could see something else, someone else. I wasn't sure exactly, but as I
looked back on the memory ... it was like looking at myself. I saw
myself reflected in his eyes.

I didn't know how I did it or even what gave me the strength,
but I managed to bind up his mangled leg to stop the flow of blood.
It was surprising because he didn't weigh as much as I would have
thought. Perhaps it was the absence of his leg. He wasn't burden-
some, just cumbersome. It took a few hours, but I managed to carry
him back to the safety of our lines and deposit him in the medical
tent. Last I heard he hadn't survived anyway. Oh well, I thought,
shit happens. Not much else I could have done ...

The recollection of those horrors of war cleared to reveal the
same man standing before me. It was the same person, but he
was different. He was ... whole. Gone were the mangled pieces
of meat and bone. Everything was now intact, healed. Then it
dawned on me, and I realised what this was all about. His smile
said it all. He was surrounded by an energy of dark pink. He
showed no sign of his injuries and looked none the worse for
wear as a result of his travails. He reached his hands out to me,
which I took in my own.

'Danke, danke für das, was du getan hast.'

I didn't understand the words but I sure understood what he
meant. The problem was, I still wasn't sure why I had done

what I did. Why hadn't I just put him out of his misery? It would have been a blessing, wouldn't it? I mean, he only survived a few more weeks, anyway. What was the point?

Just like before, the immediacy of these thoughts/questions were followed by the immediacy of the answer through the ethers. It was more than just a feeling – it was a knowing, like I heard it and understood it at the same time.

'It is because you are beginning to understand that we are all one. What you do to another, you ultimately do to yourself,' said the voice from nowhere but everywhere.

We smiled at one another in mutual recognition of what had transpired between us. As he faded into the beauty of the background, I noticed that the colour purple surrounding him had most assuredly now turned into a rich, dark pink. *Geez,* I thought, *I wonder what colour is surrounding me?*

I breathed a heavy sigh and smiled as I reclined against the large ghost-gum. *I'm glad I helped that soldier,* I thought amiably as I manoeuvred myself into a comfortable position under the tree. Then something struck me ...

'Hey, Margaret,' I said aloud into the ethers, 'how is this stuff supposed to help Michael?'

Not surprisingly, the words came like a slingshot back through the same ethers.

'Silly man, if you don't go through this 'stuff', you won't be able to help him.'

I admit to hearing her smile when she said this. She used to call me 'silly' all the time when we were 'alive'. I didn't take offence then and I didn't now.

CHAPTER 14

Michael, Age 17
Outback NSW, Australia, 1998

As a teenager, particularly a boy teenager, I understood that there were often times when I was full to the brim with things that I wanted to say but lacked the communication skills to make myself heard, let alone understood. This was one of those times. Not that most adults gave two-shits about what a teenager thought. Even Mum, as willing and understanding as she always was, had never been the best sounding board to voice my complex teenage problems upon.

My world was now covered by love. Well, at least my first exploration of this newly coloured world. Over the next months, Angela and I discovered one another – all during the demands of school and the getting of high grades, or a pass, as in my case. The months were a heady mix of skylarking, taking one-eyed shots with her old polaroid and holding hands just as the lights dimmed and the movie started. It was a strange, magical mystery tour. She was always entranced by the screen romances, and I was spellbound by the action scenes and justice revisited at the pointy end of a gun. The thing was we always held hands through the movie. In looking back, I'm not sure which was the best part. Perhaps if I had to weigh it all to balance, the scales would definitely fall to the side of 'handholding'.

I felt happy, and I'm pretty sure she felt safe. It was amazing how life's experiences could mirror our internal emotions. It was a Saturday afternoon and Angela and I were exiting the cinema complex. As I recall, it was a pretty crappy movie – a romantic drama, I think – but I didn't really care. I was holding her hand as we walked down the side street. That was all that mattered.

The three dudes walking the other way seemed to be engrossed in their own world of friendly banter, so I paid them little mind. That was, until we were next to one another and one of them, the biggest one, made some snide comment about Angela and her dress sense.

'What was that?' I said as Angela pulled at the sleeve of my jacket in an urge to walk away and just let it be. Unfortunately, that wasn't the way it worked for me. That's not how I viewed the world.

As I turned to face the big dude, I noticed he was about my height but probably carried an extra eight or ten kilograms, most of it muscle. That didn't bother me so much, but I did want to know what the other two were thinking. I noticed that both of them were standing back, slightly behind the larger antagonist. I figured then what needed to be done. I could hear Angela still urging me to 'let it go' and tugging on my sleeve with urgent intent. I heard her, but I didn't listen. I had other things on my mind.

'What was that? What did you say?' I repeated slowly so that the gorilla understood the question.

'I said,' he drawled, 'your girlfriend looks as if she would be better off with a real man. On her back or on her knees, either way would be fine with me.'

Everything from that moment seemed to happen in slow motion. It were as if time seemed to stand still. I didn't know how that happened, it just did. Then I got this flash of my Grandpa's face – when he was in the war, as a sniper – but quickly had to realign my focus. I saw the big dude's fist hurtling towards my face long before it was due to arrive. A slight twist of my body, a small dodge to one side and his extra ten kilograms only meant that he hit the asphalt harder. My right knee situated in the small of his back pretty well restricted his movements and my hand clasping his left arm at such an angle almost defied the proper laws of physics.

I looked up at the other two to ensure they were still 'rooted to their spot'. The respective looks on their faces said enough, but just in case, I added, 'Don't even think about it.'

I wasn't sure what it was, I didn't know where it came from, but the rage that seeped through every atom of my body felt almost unstoppable. I knew one more tweak would snap the dude's arm in three places. I could've snapped his bones. It would have given him a month or two to think about not insulting a woman, my woman, again. Anyway, I was just doing my part, saving her honour. That was just the way it was. I could even hear an echo of a snap of bones in my ear. Maybe it was the memory of some long-forgotten movie. Maybe it was something I'd heard when I was a kid, I didn't know.

It was about then that my senses cleared. I started to hear her. It was Angela yelling at me.

'Michael, stop! Please stop! This is not the way. If you do this our lives will be changed forever.'

I shook my head to clear the fog of rage that had filled my mind. Slowly, I released the pressure on the guy's distorted arm. His audible sigh was quickly followed by the tension of relief leaving his body, although the weight of my knee in his back probably still hurt.

'Consider yourself lucky she was here,' I whispered into his ear as I removed my weight from his prone torso.

I looked at Angela as she exhaled loudly and reached for my hand. I noticed that my hand was starting to shake. I looked at my trembling limb as if it was attached to someone else's body. *Geez!* I thought, *I wonder why it's shaking?*

The walk back to Angela's house was as full as a room full of elephants, but was mostly performed in silence.

The most important thing that bloomed from that encounter was that Angela still wanted to be with me. She didn't abandon her raging bull. We were still friends, thank God for that. I wasn't sure, though, whether she was happier with what I had not done compared to what I did do, or could've done. I supposed it didn't matter anyway. All's well that ends well! I didn't hurt him, I still had my girl and I knew I could fight. Not bad for a day's effort, really – although I still wasn't sure where that rage had come from. I pondered this very same thought as I stared at the pictures on the wall when I was alone in the quiet of my bedroom.

Matthew J. Cooper
Heaven

Finally, I had some respite from all this experiential 'life review' stuff. It was like having well-earned 'r n r' after a battle. Not that I needed a drink, mind. I didn't need anything like that in this place ... wherever I was. The sights and sounds were enough to fill me with a jubilant kind of energy – as if everything in my surrounds exuded a radiance of life-affirming and life-giving sustenance. Nothing was insignificant, nothing unimportant. Everything had a purpose. Even the colours – like nothing I'd ever seen before – were more like the seven colours of a rainbow multiplied by a factor of ten.

I rested, and my mind drifted away, not thinking of anything. No effort was required. My mind was a vast expanse of desire-less intention. I was starting to figure out how things worked in this place, so tried really hard not to think of anything. That was, of course, until I thought of something, then it all changed. I don't know how, I don't know why, but it did. All those years ago, in the pub ...

I was well behind the safety lines, and all I wanted was to be alone. The old pub had seen its share of damage but it still managed to serve pleasant tasting ale before a roaring log fire, which shed a sense of both warmth and comfort. It took away the pending chill of the northern hemisphere winter and warmed the cockles of the many souls that were feeling the ravages of their time in service to their uniform.

My schooner of ale was half full – or was it half empty – when the quiet buzz from the other patrons was interrupted by a cold blast of icy air as the front door was flung open and the pub was intruded on by raucous laughter. The three that entered had obviously frequented other such establishments for they were all in an evident state of non-sobriety, one of the three even more than the others. He was the biggest ¬– a brute of a man, with hands the size slabs of raw meat and eyes that pierced the night with flints of wolf-like intensity. Despite the interruption to the previous ambience, I turned my attention back to the schooner and switched off my mind to the heavy banter and raised voices.

The problem with pleasant-tasting ale is that it has to be refilled every so often. No more half full, or half empty – just empty. I made my way through the crowded bar and sought the attention of the over-worked young barmaid. I felt the brute's presence even before he pushed his way to the bar.

'Why don't you and me find a nice place where we can get to know one another better, eh?' he said to the lass with a lecherous smile.

The young barwoman just smiled demurely as if she had been asked the same question a thousand times before and went about her business serving and cleaning.

'I asked you a question,' snarled the brute with venom. 'I reckon it's time for you to feel what it's like to be with a real man.'

The lass ignored his jibe and placed the new schooner of fresh ale on the bar before me. Quick as lightning, the brute's massive hand wrapped itself around her delicate wrist. Her courteous efforts to retrieve what was hers proved valiant but in vain.

'I don't think the young lady is much taken with your attention,' I said quietly turning my focus towards the man-mountain. 'Perhaps it's best if you release her arm and go about your business nicely, eh.'

I felt the brute's breath on my face as he turned his malice towards me. Mind you, he was looking down from a head span higher than my own, so his breath seemed to engulf my forehead.

'Hmm, little man, and I s'pose you're the one to make me stop.'

Time seemed to stand still and the objects in the room appeared to all move with a slow-motion synchronicity. I saw his massive fist catapulting towards my face long before it was due to arrive. A slight twist of the body, a small feint to one side and the massive man was now face-first amongst the dirt on the floor. My right knee situated in the small of his back made his movements somewhat limited, and my hand clasping his left arm at such an angle almost defied the laws of human dynamics.

I didn't know where it came from, but the rage that flowed through my body in that moment was like an unstoppable force confronting an undeniable object. I knew one more tweak would snap the man's arm in three places. I couldn't help it – I was just doing my part saving the girl. I wrenched, and the snap of his broken bones echoed throughout the now-silent room. I knew his humerus was broken, but I guess it wasn't really funny. The sudden *snap seemed to bring my focus back from the rage in which it had submerged. I let go of the big man's shattered limb and noticed that my own hand had begun to shake a little. I looked at my trembling hand as if it was attached to someone else's body. Interesting! It had never failed me before under pressure.*

I didn't much hear any of the hullabaloos after that. I just picked up the schooner still waiting quietly for me on the bar, and with my non-shaking hand, took a rather large gulp. I felt its soothing graces and left the patrons and others to deal with the fallout. The icy night air hit me harder than the confrontation in the bar. I turned up my collar and made my way back to barracks, hoping that everything would be quiet when I got there. I knew I had to get a decent night's sleep as I was due to see the CO at 0600 to get new orders. The large collar of my trench coat seemed to cover my creased forehead perplexed at where the rage had come from – but at least I was just doing my part saving the girl ...

My recollection of that time in the pub made me feel both happy and sad at the same time. I never was much good at figuring out complex emotions. But I knew one thing for sure – in this place there was no hiding. True to form, my kaleidoscope appeared with a flashing, irresistible light. My hand reached for what it could not resist ...

I was instantly transported to a house. A ramshackle, untamed house if ever there was one. There was a smell of stale liquor that had embedded itself in the very fabric of the place. It filled the air with a sense of pending peril and disturbed energy. Like standing at a bar at five o'clock in the morning after all the drunks had gone home. I sure as hell didn't know why I was here, and I sure couldn't 'do' anything about what I was to witness. I was a mere observer to an arena of action. I could only stand in the corner and watch as events unfolded.

First came the yelling.

'Where are you, you little bastard?' came the rasping slurred voice. 'Wait till I get my hands on you.'

The man's rotten stench entered the room long before he did. The stains on his torn singlet looked as if they had been there for a decade. They were emphasised around the extension of his large stomach. Although it must be said, he was a giant of a man. His hands were huge and he must have weighed at least a hundred kilograms – a beast of a man with an IQ to match.

I sensed before I saw the boy cowering behind the well-worn sofa. He was petrified. He couldn't have been more than nine or ten years old, big for his age, but young none-the-less. I saw him at the same time his father did.

'Dad, please don't. I didn't mean to. It wasn't my fault,' came the terror-filled plea from the helpless boy.

I watched as the massive father removed the leather belt from the rungs of his trousers. It was a horrible beating. The boy had little left of his red-raw skin from the welts on his buttocks and back. His screams of anguish filled the air. Tomorrow he would suffer, but now it was all pain, and the father had no remorse.

I could do no more than watch in horror and scream mutely into the ethers that wouldn't let them hear. I wanted to kill the man. I wanted to stomp him into the dirt of his origin for what he was doing to the weak and defenceless child. Yet I could do nothing but watch. I felt sick to the very pit of my being. Even when the father stood panting and exhausted from his exertions, I could do nothing to help the poor lad. This was another kind of emotional torment altogether.

But then it all stopped ...

He was standing next to me. I recognised him in an instant. It wasn't so much that he was a brute of a man, nor was it his large hands. It was more the eyes that I remember. They seemed to pierce the space between us with flints of wolf-like intensity.

He didn't smile, I don't think he knew how, but he knew who I was, just not why I was here.

'You saw, didn't you?' he asked.

I nodded my response because I couldn't quite form proper words.

'It wasn't my fault, you know. It's just that I couldn't ever do anything right, that's all.'

Again, I nodded my confirmation, and at one level dreaded what was to come next, but knew that it must.

He looked at me as if I were some kind of saint, some kind of saviour from another dimension of the universe.

'I guess I have to say thank you for what you did,' he managed to rasp.

My perplexed look must have given him a little more incentive to continue.

'My arm never worked again, you know. After you broke it in the pub that night.'

'But why thank me? I don't understand? It was me who broke your arm, after you harassed that poor barmaid,' I mumbled in reply.

'I stopped, didn't I! I stopped beating up on people. I couldn't do it anymore! I only had one arm. It sure taught me a lesson,' he continued.

I couldn't resist. I reached for him and grasped him firmly by the shoulders. 'But you couldn't help it,' I said. 'That's what you were taught. That's all you knew. Your father taught you that. He taught you how to be cruel. He taught you how to inflict pain. He's the one who should be condemned, not you.'

His large chin hung loosely towards his chest, and it was all he could do to lift his eyes to look at me.

'I'm sorry,' he said between heaving gasps and a lifetime of sorrow that filled his massive frame.

My mind was a fog of words, none of which seemed to fit the occasion. That was until the same old voice appeared again from nowhere and everywhere.

'Go forward now and cause pain no more. Rise above those who would do you harm. Only by breaking the cycle can you fully express the wonder and glory of 'God I am' in your life, evermore,' I repeated.

To this day, I still do not know where those words came from.

CHAPTER 15

Michael, Age 17
Outback NSW, Australia, 1998

When someone looked back on their life, it was easy to see how things could have been different. There were times when the world turned upside down and unalterably changed direction. It had happened before. 'Perhaps, I should have ...', 'What if I had ...' or 'Maybe I could have ...' all become confined to the three baskets of 'woulda, shoulda or coulda'. The time had passed, the race had been run and there was no way we could 'turn back the clock'. I suppose if I rationalised it, that's what life is all about. Things happen in life that we have no control over. The universe assumes control with its own designs to determine how the pennies will fall. The real question is whether we can make the most of things. Turn a bad situation into good, or make sure that we are not trodden down into the lowest common denominator. This was one of those times.

Angela and I met in the same café at the same appointed hour, as was our habit. It was always the brightest day of my week. Whatever else happened during the week was of limited concern. It didn't matter if the world had poured rubbish over my head for the past six days, the seventh was always a beacon of light. I was meeting my girl – that was all that mattered. But as soon as I saw her walk past the window of the café from my position in the adjacent booth, I knew something was wrong. Her normal cheery face had been replaced by a deeply troubled frown. It was as if the weight of the world had fallen upon her shoulders and was threatening to bear her down.

'What's the matter? Whatever's happened can't be that bad,' I said in an effort to ease her burden as she sat down at the booth.

But when she took my hand across the table and tears welled in her eyes, I knew this was something more than serious. I knew it was about us.

'We're leaving,' was all she could manage before breaking down into tears.

At the same time that my chin dropped towards my chest, my mind became a disbelieving mush of tangled thoughts.

'What? What are you talking about?' I stammered.

'Mum and Dad are moving. Dad's got this new job up north. They've enrolled me in a new school. We'll be leaving next month,' she managed to relay through chest-heaving sobs.

It was as if all the air in the café had been sucked into a black hole. I could barely breathe, and my mind was spinning like it had lost control of itself. I looked everywhere except directly at my beautiful angel because I knew if I did, I would lose it completely.

'But, but ... what about us?' I managed to mumble as she wiped at her tear-stained red cheeks with a paper napkin.

The question hung between us like a vast schism.

'I don't know,' she said as another sob made her chest heave.

We discussed a lot of things that afternoon. Maybe we could run away together? Perhaps we should just get married? What if I were to go north too? Maybe I could get a job and we could live together? It all added up to a zero-sum game. The result was always the same. We were too young. She had her family and I had my mum. We had to finish school. It just didn't add up.

The next four weeks were probably the worst in my life. I moped around like a lost soul. I couldn't concentrate on anything remotely interesting at school. I only half ate my food. Shit! I couldn't even shoot straight.

Most mothers were usually pretty wise, you know, and mine was no different. She did her best to help. That is, after she was able to extract the details of Angela's departure from my tin can of pent-up emotions. She offered support in the only way she knew how. She hugged me more often and cooked up my favourite meals as frequently as she could – even when she was too tired from so many shifts. All in all, it was a shit-sandwich of a time. I approached the day of Angela's departure like a soldier going to the frontline wearing lead boots.

Despite our vows that we would talk a lot on the phone and send letters every other day, I could only stand beside the comfort of a large oak tree as I watched her face disappear in the back window of their sedan. Her last wave was like a farewell to life. I bawled my eyes out. I'd never cried so much in my whole life. I guess I should be thankful to the old lady who came walking past and noticed my distress.

'Don't worry, my boy,' she said with a comforting hand on my arm. 'Love has a way of directing its own course.'

I didn't quite know what she meant, but I did my best to smile at her wisdom before she continued on down the street.

It was funny how the universe provided serendipity in moments of distress. When I was making my way back towards home, I noticed from a distance that same big dude I had fought outside the cinema was coming towards me with his two cowardly comrades-in-arms. *Right, if this son of a bitch says one word, makes one comment, I'll rip his f**king arms off a shove them down his throat.* The rage I still had within me felt like a leaking inferno.

As fortune would have it, as soon as they saw me coming in the opposite direction, they made a beeline across to the other side of the street to avoid any indiscretions. I guess we were all lucky they did.

Matthew J. Cooper
Heaven

I supposed, when it all came down to it, I still didn't know where I was. Was this heaven? Is this what they called 'eternity'? How come there were no 'pearly gates'? Buggered if I knew. The only thing I could figure for sure was that I was where I was because I had done what I did. I mean, that's what all these experiences were about. But I did what I did as a sniper because I thought it was the right thing to do – most of the time, anyway. It was war, that's what you did in war –– although sometimes it got a bit confusing.

These thoughts and more surrounded me in layers of dense fog as I lay back amongst the field of flowers and vibrant colours. To tell you the truth, I could have stayed where I was. It was the same place as before, but different somehow. The colours seemed to be more vivid and there was a hint, just a faint hint of music on the edge of the ether. It was as if it were just at a distant point of my perception – within range but out of grasp.

When I looked back over all those thoughts that had driven my actions as a sniper, I could see how they had shaped my life. I mean, irrespective of all of my skills with a rifle, I killed because I had been told it was the right thing to do. We had been taught to resolve our differences with the pointy end of a gun – by killing one another. *Surely, there had to be a better way*, I mused? Perhaps?

I remembered going to a church service during the war one day. I think it was just after my nightmares had started. The altar was a bit makeshift, but it was wartime, after all. We made do with what we could scrounge. I remember the padre saying that 'God was on our side, not on theirs'. I mean, how does that work? I'd seen boys from our side as well as theirs cry to their God and mothers when they were in agony after a bullet had ripped through their guts. Bullets didn't discriminate. Both our boys and theirs all prayed to God when their guts were hanging out. If there were only one God, like I'd been told, then it didn't make sense that He would service one side and not the other. It just didn't add up.

All of these thoughts were starting to make my head spin. I tried my best to think of something nicer. I tried thinking of Michael. I wondered what he was doing at that exact same moment, although if there was one thing I'd learned in this place, there was 'no time and space' between love.

I looked down at my chest and, sure enough, Michael's silver cord was shimmering like a beacon. This time it shimmered with a vibrant blue colour – I felt rather than figured that he was feeling sad, really sad. I raised my hand to plunge into the cord to go and help him, but for some strange reason I couldn't move my arm. It was stuck.

'Huh? What the ...' I said as my brow creased in confusion.

Suddenly, out of seemingly nowhere, a beautiful mist surrounded me. It was both delightful and comforting at the same time, and I knew who/what it was because I couldn't help but smile.

'My love,' came Margaret's beautiful voice through the mist, 'this is a woman's work. Michael's heart is broken. You leave him to me. I know exactly what to do.' There was a slight pause as I felt her love pour forth to somewhere I knew Michael to be. 'You have other important things to do.'

At that exact same moment, the mist disappeared and my kaleidoscope re-appeared going AWOL. I couldn't resist touching the pattern of colour. I was transported in an instant to exactly where I was meant to be ...

I was called into HQ. Normally it never happened like that. Usually it was just my CO who would relay commands from on high and expect them to be followed without question. Any form of critique would be akin to insubordination. But this was different. I'd never been summoned to the 'palace' before.

Then I was introduced to the divisional commander. On first blush he looked just like any other human being, apart from the uniform and chevrons on his collar, that is. Although I did notice that his fingernails and hands were really clean, whereas mine had been bitten down to the quick with lines of ingrained dirt in the skin of my fingers, residual from my many previous missions. I suppose that's the way it worked. At least I didn't have the responsibility of ordering grown men and women into harm's way. I'm not sure how I would've gone with that. At least I knew what I knew, and I knew what the enemy looked like by the colour of their uniform.

The DC retrieved an envelope from his desk side-draw and placed it on the map-table before me. He nodded for me to open it. It was marked as top secret. The photograph of the man inside was like a photo of any other. It was a headshot of a high-ranking colonel in the enemy army.

'Private, this mongrel's name is Müller, but we just call him, 'The Beast'.' He let that last name hang in the air for an extra moment or two. 'He's an SS-Obergruppenführer and is responsible for more deaths and atrocities than we care to name. He needs to be eliminated without prejudice. His death will likely save many lives on our side, not to mention the multitude of civilians that he's slaughtered. I can't begin to tell you how important it is that he is terminated.'

My direct but questioning gaze at the DC must have triggered something in the back of my mind.

'Sir, why me?' I asked.

'Because you're the best, son!'

I wondered why he called me 'son' when it was quite obvious that we were not too far removed by age. Anyway, that's just the way things were, I gathered. Top Brass could say what they liked.

'But, how, sir? How am I supposed to get anywhere near him?'

The DC pushed aside the photograph and pointed to several positions on the map and explained that our intelligence revealed that 'The Beast' and his family would be temporarily stationed in a residence not far from the frontlines. I was assured that local patriots would get me to within a couple of kilometres of his official residence. I would have all the necessary equipment to do the job, and I would be extracted post-haste after the job was completed.

I took all this information about my future wellbeing on face value and then scanned the topographical map for as much information as I could. I pointed to the spot on the map that made the most sense.

'There, sir,' I said pointing to the exact spot. 'That's where I need to be.'

'Private, that's over a kilometre from the kill zone. Are you that good, son?'

'Yes, sir,' I said as I looked him directly in the eye.

I was pleased that the DC agreed with my estimations. At least he didn't object, although I wondered why. It might have been because he thought that colonels were more important than privates and that if I failed, we were only one private less. In the grand scheme of things, I suppose my expedience didn't matter.

Preparation and planning were everything in my line of work ... and I was good at it, meticulous, even. I wasn't feeling much of anything during this time of preparation. I just knew I had a job to do, and I knew how to do it. I didn't think of death, consequences of failure or anything like that. That rubbish made my hand tremble and that just wouldn't do.

The partisans did their job well enough, and I was now alone just as I liked it. I had my camouflage uniform, my M40, a Colt and a knife. I figured anything else was superfluous. I'd made my way without incident to the pre-designated area then got comfortable. At that distance the tripod was essential. No way in the world could I make a kill from over a kilometre without it. I was a realist, after all. The margin for error at that distance was next to nothing. My camouflage was pretty neat too. I blended into the background like a chameleon. It was all part of the planning. Everything was in readiness as the morning sun peaked over the eastern horizon. The sun was at my back, and I had a perfect view of the kill zone through what was obviously the kitchen window.

He would come. I knew he would ... so I waited. I was good at waiting. I cleared my mind and breathed in the crisp spring morning air. There was even a birdsong or two in the background to keep me entertained. I had a clear view. There was little or no wind to factor in. I didn't even have time to enter my memory banks before the action started. It all unfolded fairly quickly. The children came in first and sat at the kitchen table.

F**k, I thought, that complicates things – a lot. I didn't know there'd be kids involved, and three of them. They weren't part of the plan. The eldest looked to be no more than nine or ten years old. Then the woman followed. I figured her to be 'The Beast's' wife and mother to their children. She said something to the children because they all sat up straight, and I didn't see their lips move once more until my target entered the room and sat at the table. I didn't know why, but as soon as I saw him, the image of a hyena came to my mind. I guess that's what he looked like. His wife was busy fussing with the breakfast and was a constantly moving mark. Didn't matter anyway, she wasn't the target.

I now had him in profile. He was sitting at the head of the rectangular table. I couldn't hit his heart, but his temple would do just fine. My trigger finger twitched in anticipation. His temple was in my crosshairs. I fired.

You know, one kilometre is a long way. A bullet travels at 850 metres per second. One point one eight seconds is a long time when you are talking about killing someone, almost a lifetime, really. I should have figured he'd be the one first served. He was always going to get his breakfast before the others. The glass from the kitchen window shattered and the bullet entered the middle of her back and exited her sternum. I saw the resultant blood and gore spill over the children, and the look of horror on each of their faces.

The Beast, true to his name, took in the carnage with a glance. He dove for cover under the kitchen table. I watched mutely as the *children sat stunned with mouths open in screams that I could not hear as their mother lay dead and bleeding on the table. I didn't get the chance at another shot. There was no time to think. I knew I had to bolt lest I become dog-meat. I could only spend a fleeting moment thinking about the calamities that would befall the murderer of his wife, and I for one didn't want to end up dangling from some piano wire.*

My extraction went to plan, but only just. Another minute or two and we would have all been f**k'ed. My fear of capture and retribution faded. Thank God for the partisans.

The DC wasn't very happy that I had failed my mission. Oh, well, I thought, no plan ever goes entirely to plan. Anyway, I wasn't really worried about failing in the mission. What bothered me most were the nightmares. I couldn't sleep. For three full nights, the image of the woman's blood all over her children kept invading my dreams, and I didn't know how to stop it. The nightmares were the worst part of the whole bloody mission ...

These memories left me in a state of suspended animation, but it was only for a second before she appeared out of the ether...

Her hair was flaxen and the freckles on her nose made her look younger than the child she actually was. Or at least as old as you ever were in this place. Her eyes were deeply set as if they had been fixed hard into the concrete of her cranium. They seemed to delve into the depths of some dark, cavernous grotto. Without a smile, she held out her hand for me to take in my own. I could do nothing but accept the invitation as she led me into a thick fog, thick as pea soup.

I suddenly felt chilled to the core and shivered involuntarily in fear of approaching doom. Then, as dense as it was, the fog suddenly lifted, leaving both of us centred within a mist of light. Jewelled sparkles of refracted light assaulted my vision and distorted my sense of awareness to my surrounds. We were in a hall of mirrors, surrounded on all sides and multiple facets. I could see myself reflected a hundred times from multiple directions and perspectives. Her hand tightened in mine as soon as the images started.

I almost shit myself. 'Oh, my God,' I uttered as I watched her gentle face turn to abject terror. The images were horrendous, and there was no escape. Everywhere I looked was a horror in multiplication to itself. It would be too easy to say that we were both scared. That wouldn't describe it at all. It was a complete assault to the visual senses. Unlike some of my previous experiences in this place, I didn't 'feel' any of the pain – I just witnessed it. But that was bad enough.

I can barely bring myself to describe some of the images. There were summary executions. Beatings. Starvation. Retribution. Burnings. Horrendous experiments on children. Murders. Tortures. The thing was, central to all of these hideous images was a face with an appearance unlike any I had ever seen before. Ragged, sharpened teeth and rheumy, blood-soaked eyes peered forth from a grotesque face covered in puss-filled sores. It was the face of a beast, and yet it was human ... kind of ...

It was all I could do to drag my vision away from the horrid images and look back to the little girl. For one so young and pretty, her face was a wasteland. She looked up at me with eyes filled to their depths with pain and sorrow, but it was more than that ... she was lost. Lost within the images. She didn't know how to escape. *Oh, my God!* I thought. *This is her prison – a prison of mirrors.*

I did my best to shut the images out and kneeled in front of the poor young wraith. She was now at eye level as I took both her hands in mine.

'Why have you brought me here? This is horrible! An abomination!' I rasped desperately.

Her eyes turned to pleading as her mouth opened and shut without words.

It was then I was confronted by one particular image in the mirrors among the many. The image was of myself. I was looking through the perspective of my scope, or more correctly, it was what I had seen through my scope. I relived the sight of the blood spurting from a woman's sternum and splattering all over the young girl's face and pretty dress.

Then it came to me. I knew who she was. It was the little girl. She was a child of 'The Beast'. I was the one who had killed her mother. I missed my target. I killed the wrong person. It should have been her father, but it wasn't.

'I'm sorry. I'm so terribly sorry. I didn't mean ...' was all I could stammer as I watched the terror play across her face. I tried to apologise again, but my words only enraged her. She flew into a frenzy and started to scream. She jumped, flailed and clawed at the multiple images of her father. Her fingernails scratched at the images in the hall of mirrors but could make no impact. It altered nothing. Her screams were something I will never forget.

'Stop! Stop it, please,' I cried as I grabbed and held her with all of my strength. I almost couldn't hang on, until finally, her rage-fuelled frenzy calmed to sobs of futility.

'Look! I will try and help you,' I pleaded not really knowing how I was going to manage the feat. I stared up at the horrendous images and found no respite from the torrent. There was no safety there. But then the words came to me. I didn't know from where, but they did. My mouth seemed to play ventriloquist to the words in my mind.

'You are not to blame! He was your father, but the consequences of his actions are not for you to bear. You are a flower – a divine teardrop of God. Listen for the music. Listen for the song.'

Our eyes locked as we looked at one another still in the grasp of desperation. Then we both closed our eyes as I raised my index finger to my lips. We listened with all our might. I knew she heard it too because her eyes sprung open like saucers.

'Come,' I said as I rose from my knees. 'We must follow. We must follow the music.'

We walked and walked and as we did the mirror images began to diminish and fade. We walked some more. The music grew louder, more sublime. With each passing step towards the music, I saw the horror fade from her face. She was transforming before my very eyes. Her innocence was returning. Then it was time ...

I let go of her small hand and pointed in the direction of the music. Without words, she knew what she had to do, and I knew I could not follow. I watched her sweet smile fade as she walked away. It was enough, enough to know that I had done what I had to do. It felt right ... whatever 'right' was ...

In an instant, I was transported back where I belonged. *Far out,* I thought. *If they served beer in this place, I reckoned I would have one or two right about now!* But alas, this thought was not powerful enough for one to appear. Despite my slightest of disappointments, I exhaled deeply in thanks to the peace and safety of where I belonged.

I did my best to turn my thoughts away from the horror that I had just witnessed. I shifted my thoughts and wondered how Margaret had fared helping Michael with whatever had made him sad.

True to form, with this thought, the answer came through the ethers.

'He's fine, my love. I told him that 'love has a way of directing its own course.'

I could only smile. I knew that Margaret would set him straight.

CHAPTER 16

Michael, Age 17
Outback NSW, Australia, 1998

It all happened very quickly. One minute Angela was there and everything was fine, the next minute she wasn't. Then it was Mum's turn. One minute she was there, the next minute she wasn't. Hey, what did I know about cancer, anyway. Yes, I had heard about these things. I had read in the newspaper how so-and-so had passed away from the dreaded disease, but it was always somebody else. It was like being aware of a monster lurking in the shadows but it always attacked someone else, three parts removed in separation. Close enough to provide recognition, but far enough away to enable detachment. But this time it was personal.

I'd spent the following months after Angela's departure in a kind of listless fog. I was back to being alone again, apart from

Mum that is. Being alone had never bothered me before, but this felt entirely different. It was as if I were missing my right hand. It was like living in a vacuum. Nothing seemed to fill the void. Not school, not Mum! Not even shooting my rifle at moving targets. Bugger me! I had even missed a lot of targets. Maybe it was because I couldn't bear to front up at the abattoir with a kill and find some other cretin stationed in Angela's sacred spot.

Perhaps that was why I missed all the signals. Maybe I was too preoccupied, locked in my own misery. Whatever the reason, I didn't see it coming, that's for sure. If I had been even partially aware, I would have seen the signs: her ragged reserves of depleted energy, her face drawn with dark rings under her eyes. Maybe I just thought she was working too hard. After all, I'd stopped bringing home the odd carcass of kangaroo. Clearly I'd forgotten all about my responsibilities to the household coffers. Whatever the case, the morning of her first seizure took me completely by surprise.

It was a Saturday morning, one like any other. Mum was doing the laundry, and I was in the shed fixing my bike and itching for the time to pass through to the afternoon when I could venture forth with gun in hand. I knew this to be the case because I knew Mum had a shift on that afternoon.

I heard the crash first. The sound seemed to echo through the still air like rolling thunder. It was a sound totally out of place from what was the norm on a Saturday morning.

'Mum, are you all right,' I called from the shed.

Not hearing a reply was even worse than receiving one.

I wiped the grease from my hands as I exited the shed and called out again. That's when I saw the top of her head poking halfway through the doorway to the laundry. Blood was seeping across the white tiles and dripping like an unsealed tap on the flowers in the small garden outside.

'Holy shit!' I yelled. 'Mum, Mum, are you all right?'

I reached her and cradled her head in my arms and kept repeating the same question, but got no response. She had obviously slipped on the wet tiles. The skid marks on the floor were evidence of her feet losing traction. The gash on her forehead was open and livid and still leaking blood. I reached for whatever spare piece of linen I could and wrapped it as securely as possible to stem the flow of blood. My next thought was to call an ambulance.

The ten-minute timespan for the ambulance to arrive was like an eternity as I waited for help to show up. The aftermath was all a bit of a blur.

I waited outside in the corridor while Mum was attended to in the emergency room. I wasn't allowed in. I kept watching the clock on the wall but got really frustrated when the hands didn't seem to move. *What was taking them so long for Christ's sake*, I thought repeatedly as I paced up and down the sterile corridor. Jesus, they only had to patch up the gash on her head, for goodness sake. Can't be that hard!

Eventually, though, the doors opened and a doctor exited ...

'You must be Michael?' he asked at the same time as removing his thick glasses and giving them a quick polish.

Of course, I'm Michael, you stupid bastard, I thought. Who else would be sitting outside here for hours waiting for you to do your job properly?

I just nodded my affirmation without voicing my frustration, and asked the pertinent questions.

'Is Mum okay? Will she be all right?'

I knew when he placed a hand to my elbow and led me to one of the plastic chairs by the side of the wall that something wasn't as it should be.

I remember him telling me that Mum's head wound had been stitched and that she had received a slight concussion, the rest of what he said was a jumble-blur of words. He said they had run some extra tests and mentioned a complex name that I still can't remember. The sum total of it was that she had an extremely rare form of aggressive cancer that had spread throughout her whole body.

'Can't you fix it? What's the matter with you?' I shouted, trying my best not to let the well of tears in my chest flow through to my eyes. 'You're a doctor, aren't you?'

'I'm sorry, son. There is nothing we can do. The cancer is too advanced for us to operate.' He reached for his glasses again. 'I'm afraid the best we can do is make her as comfortable as possible.'

I wasn't exactly sure what 'keeping her as comfortable as possible' meant but I did my best to act like a man and ask what I thought was an adult-like question.

'How ... How long has she got? I mean, how much time?' I mumbled while looking at the pattern designs on the floor.

'Weeks, maybe a month or two. I'm sorry, son,' he replied, looking at me with eyes that seemed rather detached from the personal.

After he left, I just sat alone on one of the hard plastic chairs. I must have sat there for hours because I watched a lot of people go past, none of whom paid me any mind. I guess they were all caught up in their own daily struggles and didn't seem to notice a teenage boy sitting forlorn and alone on one of the hospital chairs. Maybe it was because I didn't look sick or something. They must have figured I was okay.

I watched the hands of the wall clock stand still. It took me a long time to find the courage to enter the ward where my mum was ... but then I did ...

Matthew J. Cooper
Heaven

That was interesting. I hadn't seen that one before. Or, maybe I had but it just didn't register. Like something that had been before our eyes for years, but we tripped over it because we failed to see it. I looked down at the silver cord tugging zealously on my chest. It was a healthy mix of red and pink. My instant thought was that it was a good sign, but at the same time, I noticed it also contained a strong tinge of yellow. That, I knew, wasn't fine. Intuitively, I knew whose cord it was. I didn't know how I knew, I just knew ... and I had to go there. No choice, that was just the way it was. My hand plunged deep into the cord, just as it had done before ...

She was lying in a hospital bed. A glance told me that it was one of those public wards where any sense of privacy and shame was outweighed by the thought that the person in the bed next to you was probably feeling the same thing, or too sick to care.

It was weird. I seemed to be floating above the bed in which my daughter was lying prone. At the corner of my awareness, I could even smell the overwhelming odour of hospital-grade detergent mixed with the pungent taint of sickness and malignant energy. I understood at that moment how some people's pets have a sixth sense about the illness of their master. The smell was tangible.

I knew she was awake but barely conscious. She was connected to an array of monitors with tubes extending from her arm and chest, each registering the vital signs indicative of her existence in this earthly domain. She was obviously on large doses of the best care that palliative intervention could provide, but she was pretty much 'out of it'. That didn't bother me overmuch, I knew I had a job to do. Nothing was going to stop me. Michael was there too. I said a silent thanks for his presence. He was sitting next to my daughter, Mary, just holding her right hand and stroking it softly.

I stopped 'floating' and went to her. Now, when I say I took her other hand, that doesn't rightly explain it. It was as if my hand went right through hers. No harm done, mind you. It's just that we were, like, both in a different part of the universal construction, exploring life through a different frequency. Anyway, I didn't care about any of that. I just wanted to be with her – to help her. I didn't know how, but that's what I was going to do.

I never did much believe in God when I was 'alive'. All of those times I had witnessed grown men in war crying for their mothers and their God really didn't seem to resonate with me – until now. Now I knew. Now I knew why they prayed. So that's what I did – I prayed. I held her hand and prayed. That's what Michael was doing. I just copied him.

I didn't know where it came from. I'm not even sure that I cared, but I heard the music – softly at first but then with more presence. It resonated around the room from floor to ceiling. It was the most beautiful music I had ever heard. I'm not sure if Michael heard it, but a nurse and a doctor came and went, and they didn't seem to notice it. *I wonder if the other patients could hear it?* I thought as I watched an old lady in the adjacent bed smile in her sleep. Mixed with the music was the colour green, which seemed to pervade everything in the room. I still couldn't figure how all those other people couldn't see that as well. Oh, well, not to worry! I was here to do a job, not concern myself with anybody else's spiritual awareness.

Then Mary's eyes opened with a start. She was looking right at me ... or through me, more like it. She knew I was there because she mouthed my name. Then she smiled a beautiful smile as she closed her eyes. I smiled back at her, but I didn't know if she saw that.

Michael, Age 17
Outback NSW, Australia, 1998

The interesting thing I learned about experiences with the dying is that they have so many levels, I thought as I pulled up a chair next to Mum's bed and held her hand. I knew she knew I was there. She couldn't form words, but her eyes shone with her usual love behind all the drugs they were pumping into her. I was certain that one of the levels I was feeling was denial because I kept repeating the same old thing.

'She'll be right, Mum. I'll take care of everything while you're in here. Don't worry about anything. Just get better, okay.'

I wasn't really sure if she could hear me or not, and I wondered whether my tears made any difference. But I couldn't stop them, and I didn't care who saw me. I didn't know where my next outburst came from, but it was like opening the door to the furnace room in my mind. A bit like picking the scab off unfinished business. I just couldn't figure why a benevolent God would allow a beautiful woman like my mum to suffer so. A nurse came in to check her vital signs and write something on the chart hanging on the end of the bed. She barely registered my presence, being more intent on her processes. It was all I could do to refrain from grabbing her by the throat and telling her to do something to help my mum. I suppose I was lucky I didn't. I mean, if I had done, God only knows what strife I would have been in.

After the nurse departed unharmed, I did what any red-blooded male without a clue would do. I got down on my knees.

'God, take me instead of her, please,' I pleaded until I was sure He could hear me. 'Take my miserable life. I don't care anymore! Please! Please! I promise I'll help out more around the house. She won't have to worry about anything. I'll find the money to pay the bills. I promise.'

I listened for an answer until my knees started to hurt, but the only thing I could hear was the soft snoring of the old lady in the other bed. I thought maybe I could hear the sound of nice music, but figured it must have been the hum of the freezing air-conditioning. *Son of a bitch*, I thought as I just stared out of the frosted window for I don't know how long. Nothing seemed to work. I didn't know what else to do. I think that was when Mum smiled. It was a beautiful smile, and it helped me feel a lot better.

It was kind of hard to say goodbye after another nurse came in to say that visiting hours were over. Deep down, I knew this was probably going to be my last 'goodbye', so I held Mum's hand for as long as I could before the nurse came over to help me let go.

The walk out of the ward and down the septic corridor back into the world of sunshine didn't seem quite real. Everything looked the same but felt entirely different.

CHAPTER 17

Michael, Age 17
Outback NSW, Australia, 1998

I wasn't sure which was worse, being a pallbearer or being the son of the deceased who had to listen to all of those people who didn't care when Mum was alive express how sorry they were at her passing. After all, it was a small town we lived in. Everybody was only twice removed from everyone else, yet none of them really gave a damn about anybody else's struggles. It was as if we had two hands and could walk upright then we could fend for ourselves – community, my arse!

I watched and listened as everyone single-filed past the coffin – each and all of them with sombre looks and clasped hands. I mean, where were they when Mum was busting her gut to put bread on the table for the both of us. I could only nod as her previous employer shook my hand and said how sorry he was and that she would be sorely missed. *Yeah, sure, you son of a bitch*, I thought. *And how about all of the hours she worked at minimum wages while you filled your fat-arse belly? I suppose you'll just make the other staff work harder to fill in the gaps.*

I was the last to line up to view her body. I had cut my hair and cleaned up for the occasion, but the studded collar of my crisp new shirt was too small and pinched at my neck. Someone had given me a red rose to place in the casket. Not sure who it was, but I figured I should be thankful. I could feel everybody's eyes focused on my back as I trudged forward from the front pew to the raised dais holding the coffin.

I did my best not to shed any tears. After all, someone had told me years ago that grown men never cry. So I tried my best to be a man, although my gut was churning wildly, and I could feel the heat from that room in my mind threaten to erupt at any moment. I tried my best to think of something else – something good. Like firing my M40 at a kangaroo, or the best times Angela and I had spent together. It worked to a degree. That was until I looked at Mum's lifeless form. The flashback to when I was about nine hit me like a brick. I remembered straining to look over the edge of the casket at Grandpa's lifeless body. I remembered looking up at Mum and saying that he wasn't there.

I pulled at my tight neck collar as I looked at Mum's familiar face, but it was as if she wasn't there anymore, either. The thing of flesh and bone that lay lifeless in the coffin was now just an empty vessel. It was as if the lights had been turned out in a room that was no longer needed. It was then that I saw him, just as I reached in to place the rose on her chest. At least I think I saw him, just out of the corner of my vision, in the corner of the funeral parlour, right next to the flowers standing in a cheap ceramic pot. I was sure it was Grandpa standing there. He was smiling at me. The problem was, I blinked suddenly and then he was gone. I wasn't even sure if it happened at all. It all passed in the blink of an eye.

The other thing was that I kept hearing this music. Buggered if I knew where it came from, because it wasn't the morbid music from the parlour's organist. This was different. More majestic. And the tune kept playing itself in my head like a long-lost melody. It sounded so beautiful. I made sure the whole tune took pride of place in a special room with easy access within my memory. I turned around suddenly to see if anyone else could hear what I could hear, but everybody was just looking at me as solemnly as they could when I walked back to my seat.

Matthew J. Cooper
Heaven

I just had to be there, I knew I did. I wanted to make sure she was safe. Oh, no, not safe, I guess. I knew she would be safe. If I knew anything about this place I was in, I knew it was safe. It was full of love – that was safe enough, wasn't it?

I made sure I imagined the most beautiful surrounds I could. I gave much thought to how Margaret would have arranged things. Flowers of multi-hues and scents, lush greenery with a hint of fresh herbs in the air – that should do it.

Mary looked beautiful. It was as if she'd been transformed. Gone were the dark rings under her eyes and pinched, tired expression. She was radiant. She appeared to be surrounded by an energy of purity. I almost had to shield my eyes from the glow. This was what I saw when she came running into my arms.

'Dad, you're here. I knew you would be. I just knew it,' Mary said with gleeful abandon. 'But, where are we? Where is that music coming from?' Then her face darkened and she kept glancing back over her shoulder at the tunnel she'd just left, as if she'd left something behind.

My words ran away from me as I tried my best to explain that I couldn't hear her music, but did my best to describe everything else that had happened since I'd been here. I told her about the 'life review' stuff and the kaleidoscope and the silver cord things. I'm not sure if the torrent of information all registered because I could see that she was distracted trying to listen to me while listening to the music and looking back over her shoulder at the same time.

'Dad, Dad, it's okay,' my daughter said with a smile. 'I'll be all right, don't worry. It's just that I think I've got to go. It's the music! The music, it's calling me.'

I nodded my understanding and muttered something about the silver cord between us, which she looked at and acknowledged. It was there all right. *Thank God for that*, I thought.

'If you need me … Whenever you need me near, just touch the cord,' I said emphatically as if I were now the expert on all such matters.

I wasn't sure where she went after that because she kind of just faded upwards into the beauty of the ethers, but I knew she was all right and that's all that mattered. Then it suddenly dawned on me why she'd kept looking back over her shoulder.

'Hey,' I yelled into the ether, 'Michael's okay, too. I'm looking after him …'

She didn't come back, but I heard her smile as she said, 'Yes, thank you, I know. They just told me.'

I wondered whom she meant by 'they', but I figured this place didn't hold any secrets, anyway. Nothing to hide; I guess that's what love does.

Michael, Age 17
Outback NSW, Australia, 1998

I returned home to a strange place. The garden, the shed, the rooms, everything was still the same, but it was different. I walked down the hallway and my feet echoed to the sound of emptiness. It was as much as I could do to poke my head into Mum's old bedroom and look at all her stuff that was still in exactly the same place. *When all is said and done,* I thought, *all that's left beyond dust and bones are the possessions we leave behind and the sack full of memories that keep us warm or torture us, as the case may be.*

I really didn't want to go to school the next day; I was more than prepared to play truant, given that I'd just lost my mum. That was until I heard the scrunch of unfamiliar tyres on the driveway. By the look of his uniform, the dude who was driving appeared to be someone important, and the lady passenger sitting beside him looked like the matron-lady from the 'Prisoner' series I'd been watching on television.

After I let them in, they told me they were from the department of child safety, or somewhere like that, and showed me their badges to confirm their level of importance and security.

I offered them some tea, like Mum used to do. The upshot to it all was that I told them to shove their foster-care arrangements up their arses. I wasn't going to live with some dead-beat family, that was for certain.

'... but I'm afraid you don't have any choice in the matter,' said the man in the uniform.

'Bullshit, I don't ...'

'Our job in the department of child safety is to keep you safe. It's the law,' affirmed the matron.

I told them to stick the law up their arses, too.

'Look,' I said, trying my best not to open the door to 'that' room in my mind. 'I'll be eighteen in two months' time ...' I didn't know where the rest of what I said came from. It was like it was just there, you know! Like someone had filled my mouth with words that I didn't even know were in there.

'Anyway,' I said, 'I'm going into the army. I'm going to enlist.'

I was fairly certain that's what put them both in their place because after that, all they said were mumbled platitudes like, 'make sure you enrol' and 'we'll be checking up to make sure you do'.

I slammed the door behind them as they left. The sound of the slamming door followed by the silence of the lounge room made me shake a bit. I just stood there trembling and trying hard not to cry. The best I could do was trudge over to Grandpa's old recliner chair and plonk myself down on the soft, but well-worn, leather. My hand started to tremble on the armrest. I tried to stop it but I couldn't. I stared out the window and wondered what the fuck I was going to do next.

I didn't bother going to school after that. I didn't see the point. I wasn't even sure how I was going to make good on my pledge, but I knew it was somewhere in the kitchen, so I ripped out the page in the telephone directory that was my guidepost to the nearest recruitment office. It was in the next town, a mere 400 kilometres up the road ... too far to ride my bike, so I would have to take a bus. No point in hanging around, I figured. At least, not when the house felt like a mortuary and the department of child safety was buzzing around my arse like flies.

The very next day I made the trip. After getting off the bus and making the short walk to the army's recruitment office, I told the officer that I could shoot an M40 and hit moving targets from 500 metres away. His mouth nearly hit the floor. He couldn't get the paperwork out fast enough.

When I returned home, I spent the best part of the next two weeks packing up boxes and selling as much furniture as I could. My M40 was a problem, though. I really didn't want to let it go. In the end, I figured the army would probably not let me use it, and that they would have plenty of their own, anyway. Eventually, I worked up the nerve to take it to the pawnshop in town. The owner gave me a fairly good price for it, I think. The real estate lady who came by the house was pretty helpful, too. She told me not to worry about anything as she was sure the house would sell pretty quickly. The lawyer who stopped by the next day told me that he'd make sure the money from the sale of the house would be paid into Mum's estate and that it would be paid out to me just like Mum wanted in her will. He said something about probate, but I really didn't know what that was. Anyway, he seemed like a good guy, and I trusted him to set things straight. I made sure he had my address at the army base where I was going, so I figured everything would work out just fine.

I packed as much of my stuff to take to the base as I thought was useful; the rest I shoved into boxes or gave to the charity bin. I must confess though, it was pretty hard giving most of Mum's stuff to charity. But I figured that for the best. I mean, who else would benefit from it? In reality, there wasn't much of any value. She wasn't much into jewellery or adornments. It just wasn't her style. She was a practical person, my mum. Her hard work and toil defined her as a person of substance, not the bling she could wear on her fingers.

I managed one last look at my old bike before bolting the door of the shed behind me. I didn't really feel any remorse leaving it behind. It was as if I knew that the curtain to an end of an era had fallen, and my rite of passage involved giving up things that no longer served me well.

I returned to my bedroom and gave the last rites to the room that had been my sanctuary for so long. The room looked so bare that I almost forgot Grandpa's old diary under my bed. I had taken the pictures down from the wall and placed them in my rucksack, no problem at all. Luckily, I retrieved the sacred leather satchel from its hiding place and held it firmly in my grasp, sniffing the smell of ageing leather and drying parchment. I had to open it one last time before I left. There was plenty of time, after all. The bus wouldn't be arriving for another hour.

Just like I'd done before, I opened the pages at random in the hope that serendipity would lead me to somewhere important before I entered this next phase of my life. I sure wasn't disappointed ...

The page was handwritten as usual but was somewhat more difficult to read. It was as if his hand was shaking as he was writing. *I guess lots of bad stuff like that happens in war*, I thought. God only knew what the poor man had to endure. He'd written:

I can't sleep anymore. Whenever I close my eyes, I always see the same thing. They're waiting for me ... all of them. Not sure how much longer I can do this. My hand shakes all the time now. It never did before. It's hard to stop. I've even missed a couple of times. I never missed before.

Sometimes I hear music in my head. Buggered if I know where it comes from. Sometimes I can hear it, sometimes I can't. It's like it's from some-

where just over the edge. I know it's there but I just can't grasp it.

Got a letter from Margaret today. She told me everything was fine and that she missed me terribly. She said that she couldn't wait for me to come home. I wonder whether I will be the same man that she sees in her dreams. Given my present condition, I'm pretty sure I won't be. But, I guess, that's for another day. I've got to get through the next days (and nights), yet.

Got new orders from the CO last night. Our company's being taken to the front again. He gave us this rave about our country fighting a war of defence of what was right. He went on about how we needed to take a strategic hill - a vantage point that would bring a halt to the enemy attackers. It was interesting 'cos he kept calling us the 'defenders of the truth'. We were about to attack and massacre the enemy but we were the 'defenders of the fucking truth'. It messed with my head ... a lot. I mean, there isn't any fucking truth that I can find in this God-forsaken war. We were going to mount an attack. I was going to set up a covert station like I normally did. I was going to kill people with impunity, just like I normally did - all as if we had no choice in the matter. We had to defend ourselves - defend the *fucking truth. All of this and my hand still shook?*

Shit! This war is starting to mess with my head. I'm thinking too much ... perhaps that's why I'm having these nightmares. Perhaps that's why I miss sometimes. I'm even starting to think that a bullet to the head wouldn't be a bad idea. At least it would take the pain away ... stop the nightmares.

I closed the diary, tied the leather strapping and secured the precious words in the safety of my kit bag.

Geez, I thought, *he really did do it tough! I wonder how he made it through all of that horrible stuff?* He was a beautiful man, my grandpa.

The front door behind me made a final squeak as I locked it for what I figured would be the last time. I didn't have time to think of anything else as the bus pulled up, and I had to run the last few metres before its doors closed on the end of an era and the beginning of a new one.

Luckily, I found a seat at the back on my own and could watch the old world pass by without having to speak to anyone about it.

CHAPTER 18

Matthew J. Cooper
Heaven

When I saw him walking towards me looking confused, I thought, *What am I, the God-dammed reception committee in this place?* The look on his craggy old face told me that he had just arrived. I remembered it being the same experience for me when I first got here, so perhaps I could do my best to help out some.

Interesting. When I looked through his wrinkles and sparse grey hair, I recognised him from somewhere. I couldn't quite place it for the moment, but I was certain there was some connection – something past, someone forgotten. When our eyes met, I could tell he sensed the same thing.

'Where am I?' he asked as his eyes darted around at the unfamiliar landscape. Despite my extensive range of experiences since being 'here' – wherever 'here' was – I still didn't quite know how to answer the question.

'Hey, don't worry. You are perfectly safe,' I replied as my arms spread in expanse to the beautiful meadow of flowers and abundant greenery by which we were surrounded.

'But I don't understand,' he continued. 'One minute I was sitting in my lounge room. The next moment, I'm well ... here ...'

'Yeah, I know what you mean ...' I replied as a vivid memory shot through my consciousness. I looked through his eyes as he was speaking, and the thought that I knew this person from somewhere kept gnawing at me.

'Look, I don't know exactly why I'm here to meet you, but I can't help but think that we've met somewhere before?'

'Yeah, that's what I thought when I first saw you,' the old man replied as he cocked his head to one side. 'Hey, do you hear that music? It's beautiful. I can hear it. It's as if it's calling me from somewhere, but I'm not quite sure.'

'Yeah, no!' I replied. 'I mean, no I don't hear your music. I think it works just for you, but I do hear mine ... sometimes.'

It was funny because at exactly that same moment, we both looked down at a silver cord extending between our hearts.

'Whoa! What's that?' he said in surprise.

Now I was really starting to feel as if I were a tour guide or something. 'Don't worry. These cords are really good. They connect us one to the other. The way I've got it figured is we've got a connection ... something to explore ... like a friend in need ... or something like that. The way it works is you put your hand into the cord and it takes you to where you need to be ... do you follow?'

'Wow!' he exclaimed in surprise as the wrinkles on his face played roadmap around his eyes.

'Do you want to try?' I asked, trying my best not to sound too eager.

'Yes, I guess so. If you say so,' he replied with some hesitation.

'It's okay,' I encouraged, 'let's do it together.'

Our instantaneous touch into the silver cord between us certainly did the trick. We were transported to the memory of our collective experience as quick as a flash ...

I understood as soon as we got there why I hadn't recognised him immediately. After all, we were both much younger back then and only had battle scars, not wrinkles.

I felt again the thud of heavy artillery pounding along the lines of the front. They made the ground shake like the preamble to an earthquake. It was something I just got used to in war. A bit like living right next to a railway station. The rumble and noise was always there and, I supposed, it was something my mind just tuned out after a while. It was the same with the smell. The waft of cordite filled the air with its usual heady mix of the familiar and the grind of heavy machinery and diesel fumes.

As always, I did my best to avoid people. My job as a sniper was different. I always went first. I travelled alone or sometimes with a spotter, and I had a job to do. I had to kill some of those bastards before they could take aim at our boys. I plunged my hands into the depths of my trench coat, not so much because it was cold, but ra-

ther so that I wouldn't see them shake. I was doing my best not to confront the issue, although I was starting to dread going to bed. Sleep was an instant cocktail of nightmares. At least when I was awake I could distract myself with notions of importance. Mind you, my CO had noticed my slight trembles when he gave me my latest orders. I told him it was just lack of sleep and said, 'She'll be right ... Not to worry, sir!' with over-exuberant confidence. I think he made a mental note to check up on me later, but I guess he had a lot of other more important stuff on his mind because he never did.

I ambled slowly towards a copse of trees and bracken where I could sit and chill for a while before we had to break camp. It was there that I found him ...

He couldn't have been more than eighteen. I could tell he hadn't been at the front line for very long. I could always tell. It was the look in their eyes. It was a tangled mix of bravado, fear, incompetence and longing for their mother. But there was more at stake with this young lad. The Colt sitting in his lap just at the extended reach of his fingertips indicated to a mind on the brink.

Fuck! Was my initial thought. Why me? Why do I always get the basket cases?

I did my best not to let these thoughts shine through my eyes, so I reached into my jacket pocket and pulled out a packet of cigarettes and offered him one.

At least his hand has moved away from the gun, I thought as he took a cigarette between trembling fingers.

'Do you mind if I sit?' I asked, not waiting for a reply.

He didn't respond as he placed the unlit cigarette in his mouth, and I reached for my lighter.

'What's your name, soldier?' I asked to break the ice.

'*Murray, David, Private 1st class.*'

'*You know, it's ironic, Dave,*' I said as I took a generous drag on my cigarette. '*I mean, here we are, about to place our bodies on the line for king and country ... afraid of dyin' ... and we poison ourselves with a cancer-stick at the same time. We humans sure are funny critters, aren't we?*'

I'm not sure that he saw the paradox or mirth in my clumsy philosophies, but at least I had his attention as he stared at his cigarette then stubbed it out in the dirt beside him. The silence that followed only served to increase the ground tremors and cordite until I gleaned an inkling of what to say next.

'*Look, if it's any consolation, I've been here longer than I care to remember ... and I'm not dead yet.*' He took a brief glance then frowned as my trembling hand placed the cigarette between my lips. I took a deep drag and watched the smoke rise as I exhaled upwards.

'*Have you killed anybody yet, Dave?*' I asked.

He shook his head but then squared his shoulders as if to confirm the intensity of his commitment to our cause. '*She'll be right. Don't worry about me. I'll be fine,*' he responded.

I took another long drag on my diminishing cigarette. '*Look, soldier,*' I said with some degree of conviction, '*at the end of the day, I don't give a f**k. I'm just trying to get through this shit-box of a war like everybody else. Problem is, you either kill or be killed that's the way it works.*'

'*I said, 'She'll be right'. Didn't you hear me the first time?*' Dave said with ire as he got up to leave.

I didn't know why I didn't just let him go. Besides, I really didn't give a shit and figured I'd stopped him from topping himself – here, *anyway. But something made me grab hold of his sleeve to stop him walking away.*

'I'm sorry, okay. It's just that I know what it's like. Do you know what I mean?'

He didn't respond, but I could see the tension go out of his face and shoulders.

'If it's any consolation, I've wondered whether a bullet to the brain would take all the pain away. Fact of the matter is, I shit myself every time I go into battle. But, I figure I've got a job to do. I am important ... and, I want to get home and live a long and prosperous life. You know what I'm saying?'

I wasn't sure if he nodded or was just looking at the passing ants on the ground. I scrubbed my spent cigarette into the dirt and got up.

'Soldier, at the end of the day, we've been given a life and that life is precious – too precious to take away by our own hands, anyway.'

I couldn't help but half-smile at my own clumsy philosophies. 'At least if you're going to go, go down swinging. Who knows, you might just survive long enough to bounce some grandchildren on your knee and get locked out of the house because you've come home late from the pub.'

He stared at me for a long time as if he were weighing the balance of his future possibilities in life. I watched as his hand moved slowly to grip the hilt of the Colt. My breath caught in my throat, but then I exhaled an inaudible sigh of relief when he returned the gun firmly into the safety of its holster ...

The memory passed and we were both instantly transported back to where we started from.

'I can hear the music really clearly now,' he said with a smile of understanding. 'I think I have to go.'

'I guess you do,' I replied, feeling a little annoyed that I couldn't hear the same music.

'Thank you,' he said as he started to fade into the background. 'I'll never forget what you did ... By the way, I did live to see my grandchildren grow up, and I only ever got locked out of the house once ... that was enough. The wrath of my wife was almost worse than moving to the frontline,' he said as his smile disappeared into the ethers.

Michael, Age 18
Outback NSW, Australia, 1998

Quite frankly, I found the bus ride totally boring. The recurrent stops at late-night roadside cafés only served to relieve my bladder and hunger, not my boredom. At one level, I couldn't wait. At another level, I was scared to be venturing away from the known into the unknown. I supposed at the end of the day every young adult had to go through something similar. A rite of passage or trial to manhood, something like that.

At least, as I watched the passing sameness of the landscape through the window, it gave me time to delve into my mind. I confess it was kind of nice to relive many of my moments of sweetness with Angela. The thoughts were so vivid I had to wriggle uncomfortably in my seat.

The bus then stopped at a place whose name I couldn't remember. Only one person got on the bus and despite the fact that the bus was only three-quarters full, she removed some knitting and balls of wool from her bag before placing it in the rack above my seat and asking if she could sit down next to me.

I figured it didn't matter. I'd been sitting in my own space for I didn't know how many hours, and she seemed like a nice old thing. She turned to offer me a smile as she unfurled her knitting, starting a rhythmic tick-tap of needles that moved in constant motion.

She told me her name, Hazel Murray, and that she was on her way to visit her daughter and grandchildren, just like she did every month.

' ... But you can call me Grandma Murray, dear. Everybody else does,' she said with a nice smile.

She asked me my name and what I was doing. All the while knitting away without looking at the little sweater she was knitting for one of her grandchildren. Her reply to the information of my enlistment made her stop knitting suddenly.

'That's nice, dear. I hope it all goes well for you. My late-husband, David, was in the army once you know ... many years ago,' she said as her eyes took on a rather sad, glazed look. 'He was a beautiful man, my David. He only died a few months ago. I told him to stop smoking, but he wouldn't listen.'

'I'm sorry to hear that,' I mumbled as we lapsed into silence for a while, and the countryside passed by the window at over 100 kilometres per hour.

'What about your family?' she asked out of the silence behind the sound of tyres on gravel and engine noise. 'Won't they
miss you?'

I explained that Mum had just passed away and, I don't
know why, but I added that my girlfriend had moved interstate
with her parents.

'Oh, that's a shame,' she said with a bit of shrug of her
shoulders without missing a beat of her knitting. 'Do you miss
her? Your girlfriend, I mean.' Completely ignoring the fact that
I had just lost my mum.

'Ah, yeah, kind of ...' I replied as casually as I could.

'Come now,' she said with a look of exasperation. 'Surely
you can do better than that? Do you really love this girl?'

I confess to being taken aback by her forthrightness, but I
figured it was just the old and wiser lady cutting to the heart of
the matter.

'Yeah, I mean, yes, I do ... love her, that is,' I replied directly
as I had an instant flashback of holding hands with Angela
across the table at our usual café.

'So, what are you going to do about it?' asked the old lady directly.

'Umm, err, I don't really know.'

All of a sudden the click-clacking ceased and the sound of
tyres on gravel sounded like thunder in my ears.

'Now you listen to me, young man. Take it from an old lady
who has lived a long time and knows a thing or two about love
... and loss,' she added. 'If you really love this girl, as you say you
do, you need to tell her, okay. You need to open your heart to
her so that she knows exactly what's in there. If you have any

expectation of her waiting for you until you get out of the place you're heading, you need to give her something to hang on to. Do you understand me?' she said with some degree of forceful-ness at the end.

'Yes, ma'am, I mean, Grandma Murray, I understand,' I mumbled.

'Good!' she said as her hands started their perpetual motion, again. 'Make sure you do.'

All of a sudden, the bus pulled into the next town and we both looked out of the window to gather our bearings.

'Oh, look, this is my stop,' she exclaimed as she folded her knitting into a rough bundle and reached up for her bag as the bus rolled to a halt.

'It was nice talking to you, Michael. Now, remember to do what I said, won't you, my boy. It's important,' she added.

I managed to murmur my thanks and how nice it was to meet her before she got off the bus.

I stared out the window and watched as Grandma Murray's daughter and grandchildren came running over to give her big hugs. The bus started moving again, and I resumed staring ab-sently out the window. But then it hit me like a slap in the face. I felt the old lady's words sting like a bee. I couldn't wait to write a letter to Angela on some scrappy notepaper I had in my kit bag. I finished it before we reached the next bus stop, which, fortune would have it, had a post office just nearby the road-side café. *I guess that's just how it works when things are important and are meant to happen*, I thought. A guardian angel finds you, you find some paper, you write your heart out and find a post office. All meant to be.

I told Angela in the letter that I loved her very much and that she had a central place in my heart. I told her about Mum passing away, but not to worry because I was sure she was in a better place. I told her that as soon as I finished my training, I would come and find her, no matter what. The letter was the very best I could do ... I just hoped it was enough. I figured the little prayer I said as I pushed the letter into the little red box would do the trick

CHAPTER 19

Matthew J. Cooper
Heaven

I must say I was feeling rather happy with myself after my meeting with David. It made me smile inside to know that he had lived to grow old. I remember my old grandmother telling me that, 'God works in mysterious ways' and I guess it's true, given I still didn't know exactly where I was, but I was here to meet him, anyway. Although, I must confess, I was still a little miffed at not being able to hear my own music. *I wonder why that is?* I thought. *David heard his, so why can't I? Why do I only hear it sometimes and not others? How come I can only hear it from a distance out of reach? Maybe I'm just going deaf.*

No doubt about it. Thoughts in this place were extremely powerful. They really did create a reality all of their own. I mean, off I went again to somewhere I didn't know where.

Funnily enough, I had forgotten all about my first experience in basic training ... but there you have it. I suppose there's no escape from the bodies of consequence just because I plain forgot about the event. It just wasn't possible. It didn't work like that. Every one of life's events comes back to look at you fair square in the eyes, that's for sure ...

I was lying prone on the mat of the target range, my face pointing towards the distant target. I was being trained; I was being groomed – that's how things happened in basic training. Me, however, I was different – they knew I was good. I could hit targets that others couldn't.

I caressed the barrel of my M40 like it was a thing of beauty. I'd just made another hit. The target was 700 metres away, a distance well beyond the capacity of other mere mortals from the ranks of new recruits trying to shoot a gun straight. A wry smile crossed my face after the observer – stationed with binoculars in an elevated seat behind me – told me that I'd hit the target a millimetre left of centre.

'Think you're pretty good, do you, boy?' came a gruff voice from behind me.

I turned slightly from my prone position to see my drill sergeant standing over me. His feet were spread wide and his rough-hewn hands were fixed behind his back. He looked much like a robot with a pulse.

'Well?' he commanded. 'Speak! What have you got to say for yourself?'

'Ah, Gunny,' I said with a poorly disguised swagger. 'Aren't too many people can shoot that good.'

He sniffed audibly and kicked my heel with his size eleven boots.
'*Get up, Private.*'

I arose as ordered and stood at ease before his towering form.

He looked critically at the far-off target with the hole in the centre, then pointed. '*Do you know what that is?*'

'*Sir?*' *I said with a look that didn't make sense of the question.* '*That's my target.*'

He took a half-step forward and stood directly in my face so that I could feel his hot breath pour over my face.

'*That, Cooper, is a piece of cardboard. Do you know what a piece of cardboard is, Private?*'

'*Yes, sir ...*'

'*No, you don't. You don't know what it is, do you?*'

'*No, sir,*' *I said becoming even more confused at the line of questioning, particularly given the accuracy of my shooting.*

'*That, Private, is not real ... this,*' *he said grabbing a liberal hold of my left bicep and squeezing hard until it hurt.* '*This, is real. This is flesh and blood. Cut it and it bleeds. Smash it and it breaks. Do you understand?*'

'*Yes, sir.*'

'*No, you don't. I don't think you do.*'

I could see the fire in his eyes deepen and the heat radiating from his body was enough to start a lightning strike. He pushed me forcibly backwards so that I almost tumbled.

'*Sir, I ...*'

He pushed me again so that I did fall backwards into the dirt.

'*Get up, Private, I haven't finished with you yet,*' *the drill sergeant said with a sneer.*

I must confess to feeling the heat rise from that room in my mind, but I did my level best to keep it locked away.

'Look,' he said pointing to my M40 as I got up from the dirt and dusted myself off. 'That there is the latest in modern technology. We've placed in your hands a tool of destruction well beyond anything you could have wished for in the whole of your miserable life ... or most distant nightmares. Do you understand?'

'Yes, sir. I think so, sir.'

'Words fall on deaf ears,' he said as he rolled his eyes in exasperation before turning his attention back to me. 'Observe ...' he said as he started to remove his uniform.

I must say that he was a finely sculpted man, but it was the livid scars that crossed him shoulder to sternum that caused me to stare.

'This, Private, is what a bullet can do ... and more,' he said tracing his finger along the line of the scar, 'but I was the lucky one. I survived. Many of my company didn't. I saw my friends ripped to shreds of human bone and meat by tracer bullets that only stopped moving after they pierced human flesh.'

'With that tool of destruction,' the sergeant continued, pointing at the weapon of destruction, 'you get to choose whether someone lives or dies. Whether they suffer or they don't. You can destroy a life utterly and cause untold pain and suffering to their family. Question is, Cooper, what will you choose? When you've got a human being – a person of meat and flesh locked in your sights, will you pull the trigger or won't you? Will you shoot to kill ... or shoot at all?'

'But, sir, we're at war,' I said. 'Kill or be killed. They are the enemy. We fight for good. God is on our side. That's just the way it is. Ooo-ah.'

I watched as he nodded his head in confirmation to the overriding wisdom of my conditioning.

'Yes, Private, it is! That's just the way it is.'

I watched closely as the heat went out of him and he re-buttoned his uniform.

'All that may be so, but always remember the unbelievable. Never forget the unbelievable.'

'What? Sir, I don't understand.'

'The unbelievable, Cooper, is the unbelievable horror, the unbelievable devastation, unbelievable destruction and cruelty, sadness and suffering that our beliefs about war will create.'

He continued, 'Are you prepared to accept what you currently believe in light of the consequences of your actions? Are you prepared to act, to kill and maim, knowing that the consequences will be yours to bear?'

I looked at him, suddenly realising what he was trying to tell me, but it took me more than a few moments to process the importance of what he was asking me.

'Sir, yes, sir,' I shouted as I moved smartly to attention and saluted.

'Good!' he said as he turned towards the observer behind us.

'Move the target out another hundred metres.'

'Sir, yes, sir,' was the observer's instant reply.

As the memory of my basic training faded, and now that I was back where I belonged, still perplexed as to why I couldn't hear the music, I was beginning to question the wisdom of that decision way back then. Perhaps I should have said, 'Sir, no, sir. I don't believe I can kill anybody.' But that would have changed everything, wouldn't it? I mean, I wouldn't be 'here' – wherever 'here' was. Even Michael wouldn't be where he was, either. It's funny how things worked out.

Michael, Age 18
Army Base Camp, Victoria, Australia, 1999

There wasn't much left in terms of reserves of energy after my first two weeks of basic training. I'd been marched to carry loads I'd never even considered possible. I was routinely yelled at, abused, derided and belittled. I was told what and when to do everything. I learned never to ask 'why', just 'how and when'. I'd run more miles into my legs than I thought possible. I'd learned by rote to recite the army's core values until they replaced my own ... whatever they were. I'd done more push-ups as an individual and in a collective than I ever thought reasonable. There was no time to think. There was no time to feel sad, lonely or depressed. I was either awake or asleep. If I was awake I was moving. I was learning that I had no control over anything that my drill sergeant didn't tell me to control. That's just the way it was. In those first few weeks, I learned that I couldn't do anything right, even though I tried to tell them once that I was a pretty good shot. Now that was a mistake, because 'I didn't know for shit'.

I also learned that there was no 'I' in team. I was taught that the man beside me was my 'battle buddy'. He was like a Siamese twin, only closer. We went everywhere and did everything for our buddies. We looked after our mates. That's just the way it was. I learned that 'solo' didn't work in boot camp life. There was only ever 'our' – our company, our regiment, our division and our army. If we weren't a part of 'our', we were a part of 'them'. I figured pretty quickly that 'them' were more often as not the enemy.

By the time week five of basic training came around, I was starting to fill into my teenage frame. I was growing muscle where only skin and bone had previously resided. Although, I have to say that the first time I set foot upon the firing range, I was sure that I was pretty good. I watched as the others in my company missed targets that I hit dead centre. I watched as their hands trembled as they loaded the breech and jerked at the trigger. I watched as the puffs of dust rose from the dirt behind the targets, but left the targets unblemished. I watched as my shots ripped the mid-section out of the central point. From the minimal distance we were asked to shoot, I never missed.

I laughed once at one of the other recruits as he aimed and fired and only managed to hit the target next to his own. Shit. That was a mistake.

I felt the heavy boot connect with my right foot before I turned around to berate the culprit for being so clumsy. That was until I saw who it was …

'Get up, Private,' ordered the drill sergeant as he stood firmly over me. He looked like the rock of Gibraltar as I raised myself from my prone position to stand before him. It was a very cold day, but I could feel the heat from his breath cover my face in a wave-like inferno.

'Think you're pretty good, do you?'

'Sir, yes, sir! I can shoot better than those guys.'

His eyes narrowed and pierced my soul like a laser. 'Stand to attention when you speak to me, Private,' he commanded as I snapped my heels to obey.

I felt all of the others' eyes on me as the events unfolded unhindered by laws of privacy. I even sensed the quiet that had descended over the firing range as everybody stopped firing and started watching.

'Do you know how much courage it takes to fire a gun at a target, Private?'

'Yes, sir. I mean, no, sir, I don't ...' I mumbled.

'What is it, Private? You either know or you don't?'

'Sir, I reckon it takes plenty of courage. To fire a gun, I mean.' He took a step closer into my personal space.

'You don't know anything, Private. You've got no idea.'

'Sir?' was all I could manage as I frowned, although I noticed his nose didn't flare as much as it did before.

He looked out towards the range of targets on the field as he pointed. 'Do you know what those targets are made of, Private?'

'Cardboard, sir!'

'Yes, cardboard. At least you're not as stupid as you look,' he growled. 'And how much courage does it take to shoot at some piece of cardboard?'

I reckoned I was beginning to follow the gist of his line of thought, so I replied, 'None, sir,' but that didn't prove to be the case.

'Correct! None! None at all! In fact, if you can hit a target, all it means is you can shoot straight. Isn't that right, Private?'

'Sir, yes, sir. I guess it does, but isn't that the point of the exercise?'

I was sorry those words came out as soon as they left my mouth. I watched his nasal passages flare, and his eyes narrowed into slits.

'Let me tell you something, Private. Firing a gun and hitting a target only means you can shoot straight. It doesn't mean you have courage.'

'Sir?' I answered having lost the train of his thinking, but luckily he turned away from me to direct the rest of his words and actions to the fullness of the company of avid watchers.

'Words spoken on deaf ears ... Observe ...,' he said as he removed his uniform.

Wow! I thought I was filling out physically, but this sergeant was a sculptured Adonis. But it wasn't so much that, it was the scars across his shoulders, abdomen and across his back. I could almost feel the common intake of breath from the other recruits.

'These scars are here because I lacked courage. I had an enemy in my crosshairs, and do you know what I saw?' he said looking fiercely at me, again. 'Well, do you?'

'No, sir!'

'I saw a man. That's what I saw. I saw another human being. A human being of flesh, blood and bone. That's what I saw.' He paused and took a lingering look over all the expectant faces of his new recruits. 'That same man fired first, while I hesitated. He shot three of my buddies. His bullets ripped the life from them. I was the lucky one. I survived.'

He started to replace his uniform before he continued.

'When you peer through the crosshairs, when your finger reaches for the trigger, will you be able to pull it? Will you shoot first and ask questions later? When you see the enemy's blood gush from the hole in his chest, will you know that you did good?' He turned to stare at his entire group of recruits. 'Well, will you?' he yelled.

'Sir, yes, sir?' we all yelled in unison.

'Good! Make sure you do. You and the lives of your buddies depend upon it.'

Although it happened to be me who was the prime target, I knew I'd never forget the lessons of that day.

CHAPTER 20

Matthew J. Cooper
Heaven

I sensed her presence even before I saw her. I could feel her
love even before she got near. I almost stumbled when I saw
her as she hastened forward to wrap me in her arms.

'You are doing just fine, my love,' she said as her smile
wrapped itself around my being.

'Margaret,' I stammered, 'I've missed you so much. I ...'

'Don't fret, my husband,' as she raised her finger to my lips.
'You are never without love. We are never absent one another.
We never will be. Love never dies. You must know this in your
heart.'

'But, the music. Why can't I hear the music? Others can hear
theirs. I keep having these, ah, experiences. I can feel others'

pain ... how they suffered at my hands, but I can't hear the music.'

She looked at me with a depth of love that only a divine being could display, then reached out and took my hands in her own. 'Come. Come with me. I will take you somewhere,' she said as I felt a calming breeze arrive to whisk us away to I didn't know where. She clasped me gently but firmly around the waist as we sailed off into heights unknown.

I could feel a slight resistance as we were soaring ever higher. It was as if she were moving me through layers – layers of divinity that were easy for her to pass but were more troublesome for me. It was a miracle in the unfolding. I could see colours that I had never before realised existed. I felt an all-empowering love enfold me like a divine blessing. I witnessed beings of purity, unstained by any taint of adversity. Then I started to hear it, the music. I could feel it resonate in my soul. It was the most beautiful sound I had ever heard.

She smiled at me knowingly as if to bear witness to my awakening amidst the majesty. We kept soaring, but I could feel the resistance gaining traction. She was working hard to keep us both moving forwards and upwards. Finally, she could go no further, but it mattered not. I was surrounded. Surrounded by a thousand voices, each singing praise to my arrival. I felt a complete oneness with everything and everybody – everybody that was and whoever will be. I didn't understand, but it was beyond understanding. It was more than safety because there was no need for safety. I was surrounded by the purity of love. Then from the crowd of divine beings, one stepped forward.

I let go of Margaret's hand and could do nothing else but advance to be embraced by this rapturous being. To describe this experience as pure bliss only suffices to describe an angel to a rock. But there you have it.

'Do you hear the music, now?' the being said as softly as a caress but as loud as a drum.

'Yes, yes, I hear it! I hear it!' I replied excitedly as I felt the being's eyes peer into the depths of my soul.

'This is who you are. You and I are one. There is no separation from the divine,' the being said with a smile of radiance.

'But I don't understand,' I replied. 'I have done so many bad things. I have killed ... and what about that lady? The one whose son I killed ... I mean, I have caused many to suffer, to experience pain. How is it that I can be touched by the divine?'

I felt the smile, not only from this divine being but all those who were assembled in my presence.

'Know that you are never separate from the divine. Everything that is and ever will be is touched by the essence of the divine. You hear the melody of flowers in the wind. You feel the gentle touch of sunshine on your cheeks. You see the smile of the innocent child or the gentle touch from the old and wise. All is divine and everything is touched by its essence. It is the glorious rhythm of life.'

'It is a wonder,' I replied with a shaking voice, 'but I still don't understand. Why me?'

'Why not all? For you – when you have learned that "might is not right" and that "strength is not power over, but power with" – then you will understand,' said the being with a look of complete compassion.

'Is that why I must continue my 'life review' stuff?' I asked.

The being smiled at me as if they were a loving parent speaking with a naive child. 'This 'stuff', as you so quaintly describe your evolution, will bring you ever closer to the divine being that you really are.'

'It will?' I exclaimed with surprise all over my face.

'Yes, it will. That is the essence of love. Love returning unto itself. The divine's great paradox.'

I could feel the energy of the experience starting to draw to a close and watched as the divine being melded into the essence of the totality of the surrounds. I could feel Margaret's touch to my hand that said it was time to go. I felt no sorrow, only bliss. I knew I had been touched, touched by a divine hand, but I didn't know why.

I allowed Margaret to take me. Take me back to where I belonged. It was all I could do not to wish to stay there forever ... wherever 'there' was. But I knew I could not, not for the moment, at least. I had more 'stuff' to do.

Michael, Age 19
Advanced Training camp, Victoria, Australia, 1999

I'd never been through so many deprivations my whole young life. Until now I didn't know what real physical pain was. Since graduating from boot camp and being accepted into advanced training, I'd been summarily screamed at, verbally abused, derided, abraded and mocked. I'd been subjected to deprivations well beyond the limits for most in human form. I'd waded through mud, freezing water and icy temperatures. I had learned skills of stealth, camouflage, navigation, survival and endurance. It felt awesome. In summary, I'd been moulded into a killing machine. I was tanked, and I was primed.

I didn't keep a tally of how many rounds I'd fired on the practice range but if it did not equate to thousands, then I was no judge of quantity. I was now a better shot than I ever had been. I used to count in my head how many seconds it took for my bullets to hit the target. My average was two seconds, but I managed to get up to three once. I was a sniper, one of the most feared combatants in any theatre of any war. My array of skills had been developed far beyond being able to hit an enemy combatant at a distance. I was the total package. I was only missing one vital ingredient ... I'd never killed anybody. Yeah, sure, I'd killed plenty of animals in my time. But I had never shot a bullet into human flesh. I still didn't know, when the time came, if I could I kill anybody. Would I be able to pull the trigger when the target was a human being and not a piece of cardboard?

These thoughts tumbled through the expanses of my mind one evening when lying comfortably on the bed in my garrison, quiet and alone. Unusual, really. Most often there was always the banter and jibe between other members of my company – my buddies, my colleagues, my brother's in arms. This time I had no interest in watching the camp's evening movie or shooting pool or drinking till I fell over. I just wanted some quiet time to remember how it felt to be alone.

The time had long passed when I'd felt anything like a boy. I was now standing tall at over 180 cm – in a frame of muscle and dedicated purpose. My mind was sharp and sharpened by months of re-education, re-direction and re-sculpting. Yet, interestingly, I still enjoyed delving into my childhood memory banks. This welcome time of aloneness was such a time – excepting, this time, I had the strongest urge to pick up Grandpa's old diary.

It had been safely secured under my mattress but temporarily forgotten. I reached in and pulled it from its confines and held it securely in my hands before I opened it. It only took a second to bring an image of Grandpa to mind and say a little thanks for the gift of the diary, amongst other things that he had given me – wherever he was.

The leather straps were loosened and the pages opened to whatever part the Gods of Grandpa's diary would ordain. This time it was an early part of his history. I was neither surprised nor disappointed by the result. The opened page contained another handwritten note from my beloved ancestor. It read:

Went on my first mission today. Seems as if an enemy sniper was terrorising our boys near the frontline. So far, the son of a bitch had killed four and maimed another three of our lads. My orders were to find him and kill him. Pretty simple, really! Problem was, I hadn't killed anybody, yet. This was to be my first kill. Not sure how I feel about it. I know for a fact he didn't suffer. I shot him through the head. I watched through my scope as his brains splattered all over his observer. Job done right.

At least now I know what it feels like to kill another human being. I guess I just feel ... well, empty. I located his position - all it took was patience. I waited, I watched and then I shot. Then I waited until it was safe to move, simple as that.

Hmm, I wonder if he had family? Children? A wife? I guess he had parents ... even if he was a Jerry. I wonder how they'll feel when they find out he's dead. Oh, well! I guess it's all for the greater good. I only wish I could have killed the bastard before he shot our boys.

They say that the first one is the hardest, but I don't know about that. I've only shot one. I just did what was right, didn't I! Not sure why I feel so numb, though? I guess it's because I'm just getting used to it ... at least I hope so. This is what I do. I have the strength, and by God, I will protect our boys. Kill or be killed. That's the way it is. There is no other way.

I closed the diary and allowed my grandfather's words to etch a pathway into a new room in my mind. Just in time, really, because the door to the garrison opened with a crash and four of my inebriated buddies flowed through the door in noisy banter.

CHAPTER 21

Matthew J. Cooper
Heaven

When I returned from my journey with Margaret, it was as if I was less 'me' than I ever was. A feeling of 'lightness' had permeated what was before a lodestone. It was a feeling of euphoria mixed with the realisation – a burgeoning comprehension that I was a being of the divine, if not yet a divine being.

Would you credit that? Me! A divine being? After all the bad things I had done; all the lives I had taken? How do you figure? Just doesn't seem right, now does it? Well, I guess it doesn't bear thinking about. Thinking only gets in the way sometimes. This was a feeling experience – an intuitive bypass of the mind. It was as if I was beginning to know who I really was. Not only that, I was experiencing more than just 'me'. It was more like 'I' as a totality, not just a 'me'. It was as if 'I' was 'all of us'. Yet at the same time, I knew there was more to happen. More 'stuff' I had to do.

'I wonder what's going to happen next?' I voiced into the ethers.

The excruciating pain in my stomach provided the direct answer to the honest question. It hurt like hell. I collapsed to my knees in agony and was instantly transported to the scene of the crime ...

This was war after all. Bad things happened – lots of them. I re-member this one being no exception. The poor girl couldn't have been more than fifteen or sixteen years old – a mere child in the scheme of life's journey. Yet she had to endure much more than most others as a consequence of the time and circumstances surrounding her birth.

I remember feeling pretty good about myself on the day. My or-ders had been fulfilled to the letter. I'd protected a forward party of our boys as they overran a small but strategic village on the out-skirts of our advancing western flank. We were gaining, we were winning – our enemies were in retreat. The smell of victory hung like an invisible ether amongst the heady mix of cordite and diesel oil. From memory, I'd taken out five enemy infantry and one SS commander ... now that one was a prize. One of those bastards was a real scalp. No hesitation, no mercy ... shot the bastard in the head, I did.

I felt pretty chuffed with myself as I was making my way back to headquarters and watching our advancing infantry enjoy the spoils of a well-earned victory. I even overheard a bunch of lads ar-gue over the five eggs they discovered and were to be divided amongst the eight remaining platoon members. It was about then I heard the screams ... high-pitched and terrified, surrounded by a more aggressive ruckus of banter and good-natured jibing in a language I understood.

'Nein, bitte hör auf.

'Man, is that all you've got...?'

'Give it to her. You're a pussy...'

'Nein, nein, nicht mehr, bitte.'

'C'mon, get on with it, hurry up ...'

It wasn't hard to find the source. The noise was coming from an upstairs window of a dilapidated, pockmarked building just on the outskirts of the town. I looked around to see if anyone else was distracted by the noise but the only other soldiers I saw were following their company's CO to a destination unknown. I watched as the CO glanced up at the source of the noise from the second story window. He could only give a smirk and turn to his two subordinates with a shrug and a hastened footfall. Me, I wasn't so inclined – I had to investigate.

The wooden stairs leading to the upper floor creaked under my weight as I ascended. The banter and cries grew ever louder. I didn't much see any use for my M40. The limited confines of the stairs and passageway were too close for optimum efficiency. My Colt would do just fine. Just in case.

No need for security from whoever was inside; the door was ajar and swung open easily with a gentle shove, but I wasn't at all prepared for what I saw. The bottle of whisky was all but empty, having been passed around eager hands as they excitedly watched their colleague's violation of the young girl. I felt a lightning bolt of pain pierce my gut as I took in the scene unfolding before me. It wasn't as if I had been hit, or anything, it was just that the pain was a shock to my proper sensibilities. An atrocity in the unfolding, a violation of the spirit of humanity, a young woman in distress, and I was now a witness.

The Colt I had cocked and raised in readiness when I entered the room was now lowered to neutral when I saw it was our boys – all four of them. But I kept the safety off, just in case. The look of horror and pain on the poor girl's face as she was being raped is something that will be forever etched in my mind.

One of the lads was amidst re-buttoning the zipper of his trousers while two others were eagerly waiting their turn. It was easy to tell because the bulge in their trousers attested to the obvious. The fourth had evidently just commenced his abuse and was panting and thrusting feverishly over his captive fraulein.

The instant I entered the room became a moment frozen in time. We all looked at one another in anticipation of the next unfolding moments. But for me everything flowed in slow motion. I watched and just knew the one holding the near-empty bottle of whisky would be the one to break the seal off the moment. He held out the bottle towards me as a peace offering.

'You can have some of this if you like, but the girl's ours, I'm afraid. Spoils of war and all that,' he said with a lecherous grin.

I felt my trigger finger itch slightly as I watched the one remove his hand slowly from the zipper of his trousers. The hand moved ever so slowly from his pants to his sidearm. The flick of the button on his holster offering ease of access to the gun echoed in my ears. But, as I said, for me, everything happened in slow motion, just like it does in the movies. It took only two easy paces to reach my destination.

'Problem with Colts,' I said amiably as I placed the pointy end of my gun into the ear of the soldier in mid-thrust, 'is that most people couldn't hit shit from over 25 metres. The problem you've got, as I see it,' I continued, as I watched the other's hand inch closer towards the hilt of his weapon, 'is that I'm a lot closer than that.' Mind you, at least this one had stopped thrusting by this stage. His grunts were getting on my nerves, anyway. I guess it must have been the pressure of the Colt's barrel in his ear that made his excited eagerness turn somewhat more flaccid.

I was quick. I was good. I knew that, but they didn't. When I fired the Colt, the noise reverberated around the small room like an echo in a grotto. The worse part though was the scream. I couldn't have cared less about the other soldier's pain after the index finger from his right hand exploded in a mass of blood and rendered tissue. The fact of the matter was he just wasn't quick enough. I'd managed to remove my Colt from the open earlobe of the petrified rapist and shot off his buddy's finger before he could release his weapon. No problem with the others, I thought. They were frozen to the same spot on the floor.

'Son of a bitch,' spat the injured through pain as he clasped his hand in agony. 'What did you do that for? We're on the same side for Christ's sake.'

I looked at him sideways but remained resolute. My focus turned to the girl.

Words weren't needed as I motioned with my head for her to put her dress back on. I was thankful that she did so quickly as she told me everything I needed to know with her eyes as she hastened from the room. That was good because I could then turn my attention back to the source of the original inquiry.

'Yeah, I reckon you're right. We're on the same side, all right,' I said as I took a good look at my uniform. 'Difference is, I respect my uniform ... Plus, I reckon Christ is notably absent from what you boys were doing, don't you think?'

I cocked my head to one side in anticipation of a response but didn't get one. I guess they were overwhelmed by the soundness of my logic, or maybe they were just shit-scared in case I decided to exercise my right of privilege with the Colt. The shot soldier's moans of pain were really getting on my nerves, so I motioned for one of the others to go help bandage his buddy's hand. Oh, well, I thought, at least he won't have to have the bullet removed – it went right through. The thought brought the trace of a smile to my face.

'I figure we're at a stalemate, don't you reckon, lads?' I said after the wound had been bandaged and the moans had subsided. 'I mean, I'm happy not to report your misdeeds if you're happy to suffer in silence – about the wound to your hand, I mean. Do we all agree?' I said pausing for a moment. 'Hey, think on the bright side. You might even get a ticket home. I guess you can't fire a gun without a trigger finger, can you.'

With that said, I touched my cap in salute and took my leave making sure that I didn't show them my back on the way out ...

'Who are you,' I asked in surprise when I turned to find a lady waiting for me as I shook my head to clear the memory. She just seemed to have appeared out of thin air.

To say she was gracious would not do her elegance any justice. She stood not more than five feet and five inches tall with steel grey hair cascading around her placid face. It gave her an appearance of total grandeur. There was something about her that resonated love incarnate. She was dignity personified as her smile drove an arrow through my heart.

Her hand reached slowly for my own. I couldn't help but take possession. You know, it was interesting! I still didn't know how a lot of things worked in this place, but I swear I could hear her sweet voice echo through my being as clear as a bell – but her lips never moved once.

'Do you not remember me?' she said.

I knew my memory banks were fairly full, and I knew there were places I couldn't go and couldn't remember – this was certainly one of those times. I tried, but only drew a blank of recognition.

'No,' I replied. 'I'm so sorry, I don't. But if it's any consolation, I'm really happy to meet you. I don't want to be rude or anything, but there is something about you that, well, makes me feel happy to be with you.'

She smiled again at my clumsy revelations. 'Come,' she said, 'I want to show you something.' Her hand felt like the caress of silk across my own as the ethers parted to reveal a grand vista of what can only be described as a field of happiness. It was a scene filled with the joyous laughter of children at play. Gay garlands of flowers bedecked a playground of swings and roundabouts. All the children were safe and well, and they were filled with the sort of innocent happiness and gentle excitement that only children can portray, untainted and unstained by the dirt of complexity.

'This is beautiful,' I exclaimed as I watched upon the wonder of purity in action.

'Yes it is,' replied the lady, 'and it's all because of you.'

'Me?' I said, as my surprise hit the profound button. 'But, how? Why?'

She pointed to one of the children at play. A beautiful young being with golden locks that fell like sunshine over her forehead and shoulders. 'Do you see that girl over there?'

I nodded.

'She is my daughter. She died when she was only five years old.'

'Oh, I'm sorry,' I mumbled as I watched a gentle smile play itself across the beautiful lady's face.

'Oh, don't be,' she replied. 'It's okay. She is perfectly safe and well, as you can see.'

'Yes, she is,' I replied, 'but I don't understand. What does it have to do with me? Why are you showing me this?'

The lady turned to me and peered into my being with a depth of knowing much more than I did. 'If it had not been for what you did, all of those other children that you see would have suffered terribly. They would have experienced much more than life should beset upon the young and the innocent.'

I looked at her strangely but in anticipation of further revelations to ease my naivety.

'After you saved me; after you shot your own soldier in the hand, months later, I gave birth to my beautiful daughter, but, as I told you, she died when she was five years old.'

'But how can that be good?' I said as I squeezed her hand a little tighter.

'That was when I started ... after she died, I mean. My sorrow and grief drove me to revelation. I was determined to find a cure. I wanted to find a cure for the disease that took my beautiful daughter's life. So that's what I did.'

'Don't you see?' she added, 'By saving me from those men, by not letting them use me and dispose of me like a piece of wasted humanity, I was able to save many children. The consequences of your actions saved a multitude of others.'

My dawning smile broke open in recognition of saving graces.

'Do you mean to say that my skills of marksmanship came in handy for once, not just for killing?' I replied somewhat demurely as I almost squeezed the life out of the lady's hand. She beamed a radiant smile at me.

'Do you remember the pain you felt? The pain in your abdomen?' she asked to my further surprise.

'Yes, of course. It was awful,' I replied, remembering the acute pain.

'That is what is called 'the pain of righteousness'. It stabs you with a bolt of knowing – the undeniable feeling in your being for what must be done and when it must be done. But it takes courage. No hesitation, no second thought – all courage. Do you follow?'

'I do,' I replied eagerly.

'And do you know that few among many have such capacity to do what must be done because it is 'right'?'

'Yes, yes,' I replied excitedly. 'I guess that's what I did, didn't I?'

'Yes, you did! And did you know that the highest form of love is not to sacrifice 'the one for the many', but rather, to 'save the one to save the many'? That is the way of pure love.'

She said these lingering words with a smile that will reside in my consciousness for an eternity.

'I must go now. They are calling me. I can hear their music.

'But, wait ...'

'You too will hear it soon,' she said as her form melded into the beauty of the background and I could see her no more ... but her smile lasted a long time and was well secured in a special room of my being. I was pretty happy that I saved a woman in distress. What I was only just now beginning to realise were the myriad consequences to my actions. I could not have imagined this in a million years of earth time.

Michael, Age 19
Advanced Training camp, Victoria, Australia, 1999

I finally received my first recreational leave. Two weeks of respite from the constant physical training and I knew exactly where I was going. I was heading north to visit Angela. The letters I'd received from her told me everything I needed to know.

She told me that my letters had made her cry and that she felt the same way about me. That part really did bring a smile to my face. I was reading her most recent letter while lying on the bed of my garrison, and the ever-sombre Private Kowalski asked what I was so happy about. I just told him to f**k-off and mind his own damn business.

Angela mentioned that she had settled into her family's new home in the city of Brisbane, but missed the wide-open expanses of our former rural township. I guess that's the way it is when you move to a big city. Lots more people but a lot less community. She said that she had started attending a new college and was studying botany. Now that made a lot of sense given her predilection for things green and floral. She asked me to write again soon and signed the letter with three big kisses. That brought another smile to my face, but Kowalski didn't ask why this time. *Anyway, bugger writing*, I thought. *I will just turn up. That should surprise the heck out of her.*

The bus ride north was a long way. It took up a lot of my leave. But I didn't mind; it gave me plenty of time to rehearse what I was going to say to her when I got there. *Blimey, I hope she likes the new me*, I mused as I looked at my reflection in the night-time bus window, *After all, I'm a man now*. I couldn't help but feel proud as I looked at the size of my biceps in the window. I was tanked and dangerous. My self-satisfied musings were interrupted only when the bus pulled into a roadside café to refuel and refresh. I got off after everybody else but still managed to find a booth to myself. That way I didn't have to converse with anybody except the waitress and that was only to order coffee and eggs over-easy, just as I liked them. Even so, she smiled at me nicely and commented on my uniform, asking if I was in the army. I figured the question was a mite rhetorical but answered pleasantly to the affirmative anyway.

She went off to place my order after filling my cup, and I was able to examine the swirling blackness and inhale the tangy aroma of the freshly brewed beans in peace ... at least for a few minutes, anyway.

The door of the café opened abruptly to allow a blast of hot air and three, what I guessed must be local lads just coming off shift, to enter. They were all wearing the same oil-stained coveralls. They sat on the stools facing the counter and cast a cursory gaze over all of the patrons in the café. I felt the gaze of one of them, the big one in the middle, linger longer over my booth than it did for the other patrons, but I was busy looking into the depths of my coffee for any sign of life, so I didn't pay it any mind.

The eggs looked perfect, and my stomach growled in anticipation as the waitress placed them before me. I looked up from my coffee with a half-smile of thanks.

'Going to be in town long?' she asked as she lingered at my table.

I figured that it was another rhetorical question given that I had just gotten off the bus, but I answered politely and told her I was only passing through.

'Pity,' she said with a slight shrug of her shoulders and twinkle in her eyes. 'It'd be nice to have an army boy in town for a change, not just these brontosauruses,' she said glancing over her shoulder at the three lads. The waitress moved back to her other customers with a flourish, which was good because I could return to my coffee and start a demolition job on my eggs.

But you know how it is – nothing good ever comes easy in life. It's as if all you want to be is left alone to move between points on the compass, but then something happens that tosses you in the deep-end of someone else's dilemmas. The raised voice from the biggest of the three lads at the counter was really annoying, particularly as I hadn't had a chance to finish my eggs. I guess it was the fact that he called the waitress a slut that got up my goat. I even felt this sharp pain in my gut, which was kind of strange. After all, the girl was just being friendly. No need for anyone to be so rude, particularly when she was just being nice and, more so, when she was a lady ... now that just wouldn't do.

I placed enough cash under my empty plate, figuring that I didn't want to wait for the bill to be delivered to my table. After all, the girl was obviously feeling upset because she was trying her best to hold back a rising flood of tears in the kitchen. I moved up close to the counter and asked nicely if the three lads wouldn't mind stepping outside because I wanted to have a word with them.

Now, I knew how these things worked. Words got said, meaning got misconstrued and tempers flared. That's all perfectly understandable. What I couldn't figure, though, was why, as I was following the three into the car park outside the café, 'that' door in my mind opened really quickly. It felt like a door to a blast furnace had blown open as the resultant flames shot through my body like a blowtorch.

Mind you, at first, I did my best not to really hurt them, although they were, all three, in various degrees of pain lying in the dirt of the car park after our little altercation.

'You son of a bitch,' said the big lad as he gasped for breath and started to raise himself from the dirt.

Now that really did trigger something out of 'that' room. My mum certainly was no bitch. She had been the best mum you could ever have had, as far as I was concerned. I wrenched the big one's arm backwards until it really didn't want to move any further. I knew one more tug would shatter the limb and cause him, not me, a great deal of pain.

Moments in time are like a lot of things, they come, they go and then they're gone forever, most of them forgotten. But this one was different. This moment seemed to linger a bit longer and it was full, I mean, really full of important things. I could hear the words as if they were spoken directly into my ear, but I swear there was no one else around. There were only the three lads and me – and they were kind of occupied with pain. But the words were clear enough, that's for certain.

'This is not the way! This is not the way! Violence only begets violence. I know now. I know the consequences.'

I looked around again to confirm that no one else was there. It was then, in that rather full moment, I recognised the voice. It was a voice I knew – a voice from somewhere in the past. Then, right at the end of that full moment, I recognised it. I knew who it was. It was Grandpa.

I let the pressure off the big one's arm and heard an audible sigh of relief as a consequence – and I suppose I was lucky too. The bus gave a toot to signify its departure, so I brushed the dirt from my hands and strolled easily back towards the open door before getting back on board.

I glanced back towards the door of the café as I stepped on the bus and saw the waitress give me a wave and a nice smile as I moved towards the back. I waved back.

As the bus pulled away from the café, I wondered absently what would happen to the nice girl behind the counter. *I hope she makes something of her life*, I thought.

CHAPTER 22

Michael, Age 19
Queensland, Australia, 1999

I arrived at the crowded Brisbane city bus terminal and took the letter from my pocket, which had Angela's address written on the back. Fortunately, the nice man behind the counter was able to give me directions to the proper location. We'd arrived early morning, so I figured a brisk walk of a few kilometres would do me the world of good after sitting on the bus for so long. The early spring morning and the gentle breeze was a blessed distraction from the smell of diesel and roar of the engine.

The walk only took an hour, and I was able to figure out what I was going to say to the girl I loved and why I hadn't bothered to write to tell her I was coming. I checked the street sign against the information on the back of the envelope to confirm that this was indeed my ultimate destination. I peered resolutely down the leafy suburban avenue for the number twenty-four.

I'm not sure what it was, or where the feeling came from, but my feet started to feel heavier with each step I took towards the right number ... numbers 2, 4 and 6 came and went, and it felt as if my boots were filling with lead. Mind you, I did manage to get to number 20 before stopping altogether. From that distance, I could even see the number 24 on the letterbox outside the house. It certainly looked like a pleasant sort of house, much in keeping with the others in the street. I checked myself to make sure everything was in order. My uniform was crisp and well ironed despite the ravages of the journey. My hair was cropped and clean and my fingernails had been scrubbed just like Mum had taught me to do. I couldn't figure it out. Why couldn't I move any further?

I looked down and noticed that my right hand was shaking slightly. I looked at my hand like it was an alien part of my body. It had never shaken like this before. Not in any of my more physical confrontations, nor in the thousands of rounds I had fired at inanimate objects and faunal targets. It just didn't make any sense.

I reasoned that it was the sight of the children's park opposite the number 24 that enabled my feet to move again. I managed to take up a position a few metres away from the play swing and roundabout, just beside and behind a large gum tree. I made a soft padding of dried leaves and lichen and sat down in observation of any signs of life from number 24. It didn't take more than fifteen minutes before I saw her father exit the front door, get into his car and drive away. I guess he was going to work because it was still a workday in the big city. I returned to the silence surrounding my observation post, and it could not have been thirty minutes of watching and waiting before further activity occurred. Although, I must confess, time had lost its relevance, and its passing was only evidenced by the diminishing shadows of the playground swings and rounda-bout. The elegant lady who appeared at the front door must have been Angela's mum because the similarities were striking. The only discernible difference was the slight tinge of grey in her hair and the crow's feet around the delicacy of her eyes. I could see the beauty that would become my Angela when the years passed but failed to condemn.

The woman turned to smile and voice words that I could not hear to someone within the confines of the house before clos-ing the door gently and making her way along the street towards what I could only discern as distant shops.

Well, at least I know that Angela is in the house and her parents are gone, I thought as I rose from my bed of lichen and leaves. Yet I was still rooted to the same spot. I still could not move. My legs turned to jelly at the same time as my throat constricted and my palms began to sweat profusely as soon as I attempted to walk. It just didn't make sense. Why was I so afraid? What, indeed, was I afraid of?

It was all I could do to fall back to my original position and stare at the wind whispering gently through the trees and draw my eyebrows together to berate myself for my lack of courage.

'Far out! What's the matter with you? I love this girl ...,' I said to no one but the tree and the listening birds, who were too busy with their own lives to care about my insecurities. I closed my eyes and tried to bypass the inner conflict of self-doubt and self-loathing to reach inside my mind for some kind of a reference point to the mystery. I went searching along a myriad of corridors and previously unknown alleyways of my awareness in search of understanding – but every door I tried was firmly locked. I brushed the sweat from my brow with the palm of my hand in increasing agitation but could do nothing about the uniform that was clinging to my back.

I felt a chill wind whistle through the corridors of my mind, one that I had never felt before. I shivered involuntarily as it met my sweat-soaked uniform and seemed to echo with unhinged words I had neither previously heard in the whole of my life when inside my own mind.

'You're not good enough for her.'

'You're a trained killer. She's an angel.'

'You'll make her life a misery.'

'Get out of here, fast.'

'Help me, please,' I screamed inwardly as my mind whirled down another of the myriad corridors as I kept trying doors that refused to open ...

Matthew J. Cooper
Heaven

I was still firmly entranced by the lingering smile of the beautiful lady and was quite content to rest in the warmth of our encounter when I felt the now-familiar tug upon my chest. Sure enough, the silver cord that I knew belonged to Michael was chiming vividly and needed urgent attention. This time I knew what it was about, and I knew I had to help. I plunged my hand into the shimmering light. In an instant of a heart's beat, I was transported ...

I could feel his tension. I could sense his dilemma. I watched as his mind darted in agitation along a myriad of pathways and closed doorways. It was as if I was in his memory-mind, but I could not yet discern the nature of the trouble he was in. I was here to help yet I did not know what to do. I reached out to him, but he could not see me. I tried to speak but the words fell into deafening silence. I could feel his anguish, his fear and self-loathing, yet I could not respond. It was as if we were too much alike to help one another. It was then that I heard her voice. Softly at first, then, as I strained to listen through the ethers, the words brought clarity. The voice that caressed my soul sounded familiar, but it wasn't until I heard the words that I knew their source.

'My love, tell him that love will always overcome fear.

'Tell him that love, compassion, caring and acceptance begins with the self.

'Say that, within him, he has the limitless capacity to create and inspire a love for and through others.

'Tell him, tell him, quickly! You must! Before he gets lost in his mind ... you must hurry.'

I stopped. I heard. I understood, all in an instant.

'Michael, Michael,' I spoke earnestly into the ethers. 'I am here. I am here.'

I watched as he stopped running in his mind. I watched as he looked around to find the source of the words I spoke, but could not discern their origin. I saw his smile of recognition – in recognition of my voice. I watched as the words I spoke entered his being like a transfusion of love. I watched as I saw the lines of his face change from anxiety to joy. I smiled when he smiled. I heard as he mouthed his gratitude. It was then I knew my job was done. I knew that he knew. I knew he would do what he needed to do. He would do what served him best, not just what was right.

I watched as he left his insecurities behind. I watched as he arose eagerly from his soft bed of lichen and leaves. I saw as he walked briskly to the front door of the house marked with the number 24 and knocked firmly on the door. I looked on as a beautiful young woman opened the door to the next part of their lives. I saw the plate and dishcloth she was holding fall to the ground and smash. I saw the surprise on her face morph into a glow of eternal love. I smiled as they came together and the tears fell down their faces and the smiles lingered over their love. My job was done. For now.

CHAPTER 23

Matthew J. Cooper
Heaven

I was back. I was back where I belonged. I still wasn't quite sure where, but I felt it as a belonging. In fact, it was beginning to feel like home – much akin to a cocoon – of love. My recent experiences with Michael and the beautiful lady had shown me plenty – plenty about love, plenty about compassion and understanding and empathy and all of that stuff. I was beginning to feel, well … whole. It was as if I was beginning to realise, to experience 'who I really was', or more precisely – who I really am.

I reclined on a soft bed of lichen and watched above as the lights and colours bounced around within the playground of my senses. At a near distance, I could even hear the soft whisper of music. I strained hard to hear. It was there all right. It was beautiful. Soft, enticing, yet still at a distance. It was at that precise moment that I touched my kaleidoscope and was transported into another memory. *Geez,* I thought, *here we go again* ...

The orders seemed a bit vague, I must confess. After all, we were winning the war. That was obvious. We'd broken through lines of enemy combatants. They were in retreat and the word filtering down from on high was that the war would be over in a matter of days. Thank God for that. Finally, the horror would be over. I had survived! Intact physically and still mentally sound. That's why the orders didn't make much sense.

The CO, as usual, gave proper coordinates for my position and told me to 'clean up' any stragglers. Stragglers? Clean up? What the hell did that mean? Kill any bastard that was trying to get back home? Why the hell for? My job was to help win the war. Kill the bastards before they killed me, or any of our lads. I had done my best – that was certain. I'd paid my dues, paid the price of admission and the consequences thereafter. I'd done what was right, no doubt about that. We had won! My kill scoreboard was a total of plenty – that was for sure. Yeah, I was a killer, but I wasn't a murderer. Revenge was not on my menu for dessert.

I looked curiously through tired, bloodshot eyes at the CO as he sat at his rickety wooden desk under the feeble light of the lamp. He was pointing fixedly to the spot on the map where I was ordered to set up.

'But, sir, I ...'

He looked at me sternly before I could continue, cutting any objections before I could find a further voice. It was a rather full moment for both of us. I could see in his eyes an endless expanse of exhaustion. So many good men dead – under his watch, at his command – so many burdens of guilt to bear for a lifetime and God knows what thereafter. Whereas, for me, leeching from one of the rooms in my mind, I could hear a hundred voices all crying out together, 'Bring out the bodies! Bring out the bodies!'

'Just do it, Private. No questions. That's an order.'

I guess the problem with being a private is that you are on the bottom of the shit-pile ... and shit flows downhill as we all know. The best I could do in objection was to sneer and exit without saluting. That'll teach the bastard. I pondered my lack of respect as I trudged back to my garrison to collect my gear. Hopefully, this is the last time I've got to follow orders from these assholes, *I thought as I collected my camouflage gear and rifle.*

I was lying on a slightly damp mixture of leaves, mud and lichen. My helmet, face and uniform were entirely covered in muddy-brown ooze. Only my eyes were clear to view my objective through the scope's aperture. I felt the chill of the early morning breeze as it drifted its way across the desolate expanse before me. I waited in silence for an eternity, so long in fact that my neck and shoulders started to cramp.

'Bloody stupid orders,' I said to myself. 'What's the point?' Then there was movement.

Distance approximately five hundred metres, three enemy combatants, all in abject retreat. Bedraggled uniforms, slumped

shoulders and haggard visages were the sum total of this human
refuse. I watched them carefully through the scope. They were dis-
traught, defeated and unarmed, as far as I could see. The fight had
obviously been belted out of them.

I fixed the last in line through my crosshairs, just like I had been
taught to do. Shoot the last in line, that way his mates turn around
to see what's happened – elementary really. It gave me a chance to
reload and kill the others. I looked at my target and then at my
hand ... it was visibly shaking. I sensed my finger itch as I felt the
cool metal of the trigger. I took a deep breath, squeezed and fired.

The puff of dust and echo of reverberation of a fast-moving pro-
jectile impacting dirt was enough to make the three of them dive for
the nearest cover – which wasn't much, to be sure. I could have
killed them all twice over if I was of a mind to. I watched as the
three pairs of eyes darted a petrified dance to find the source of the
killer projectile. One of them pointed in the vague direction of my
hiding place, but they really had no idea where I was. They were all
too scared.

I sat, silent and unmoved, as I pondered why I'd missed on pur-
pose. I watched as the three distraught soldiers made a dash for the
nearest ravine about one hundred metres to the west. I watched but
didn't intervene. I let them live.

So I felt sorry for them, I thought. Oh, well, what the f**k, the
CO would never know. F**k him, anyway ...

The moments of memory passed, and as I shook my head to
clear the aftershock, I was confronted by what could only be
described as a 'being of light'. I guess some would call it an angel. I mean, when 'alive', I saw these pictures of angels as

someone with wings, all dressed in white with hands held out in divine greeting. This certainly was not the case. The best I could describe this luminous being was – like a little child. An innocent child, untouched by the stains of life's lowest common denominators.

I could not tell whether it was a little boy or a little girl. In truth, it really didn't matter. All I could tell is that the light that surrounded this being from heaven was as nothing I had ever seen before. I almost had to shield my eyes from the glare of radiance. And then there was the music. Beautiful music, which seemed to flow through, or be a part of, this being of light.

'Who are you?' I managed to mumble.

The angelic child only smiled and held out its hands for me to clasp. It was like touching the finest quality silk, the softest talcum, all in one. I felt its power. But it wasn't a power over – it was a power for. I felt it course through my veins and fill my heart to bursting. It was as if the whole world of love had been poured into my being.

I watched as the angel's eyes smiled, but I swear its lips did not move as it spoke. 'Compassion never ends, love never stops. Only in the world of man is goodness restricted,' it said.

'But, why me? I don't understand ... I killed so many!'

'You deserve it ... Let me show you,' said the angel as it waved its free hand forward in a kind of circle. What opened before me was a grand vista, something like a widescreen cinema. All I could do was stare in awe and watch as the scene unfolded ...

I saw on the widescreen as the three men I'd spared made a dash for the ravine I told you about. But then the scene changed, or more particularly, it continued.

The three men dived under the cover of the ledge, well secured from the possibility of any further bullets. They were each panting feverishly and the fear in their respective eyes was as tangible as the slush they were crouching in.

'Gott in Himmel,' said the first as he turned in panic to his similarly distraught comrades. 'Wenn ich jemals aus dieser Scheiße rausgehe, Ich werde Priester werden.' Loosely translated, I believe he said that if he ever got out of this shit, he'd become a priest.

The second equally petrified human responded in kind, 'Ich werde dafür sorgen, dass meine Söhne niemals in einem Krieg kämpfen müssen.' Similarly translated, he said that he was going to ensure that his son never had to fight in a war.

The third of them made his own vow, 'Ich werde meine Kinder von ganzem Herzen und ganzer Seele lieben.' Translated meaning is that he would love his children with all his heart and all his soul.

As the image faded of the three, it was replaced by a three-way split cinematic screen portrayal.

The first screen showed a man whose face I barely recognised. Gone were the frightened eyes and the dirt-encrusted, deeply furrowed forehead. It had been replaced by a beatific look from eyes that were experiencing the love of God as he ministered to his flock of parishioners. The second screen displayed a young man – obviously a politician – speaking about how there must be peace between nations. In the front row of the auditorium sat an old man in a wheelchair. The old man had tears of joy in his eyes as he watched his son orate words that filled his heart. The third screen was the most beautiful of all. The grey-haired old man was lying on his bed, obviously near to his last breath on earth. He was surrounded by his family of children and grandchildren, all with tears in their eyes. They were all there to say goodbye to their beloved father and grandfather ...

I turned my back from the screen to face my own angelic being with my chest full to bursting with love. The beauty of his/her smile was like nothing I could describe.

'Do you see what you have done? Your compassion woke them up. You reminded them of who they really are. Your choice towards compassion was what they needed to allow them to follow their highest path,' he/she said.

'I did?' I replied with evident surprise at the reality of my course of action.

'Yes, and more did you do. You see, the fastest path to who we really are is often the discovery of who we are not. This is the greatest gift of compassion.'

Upon these words, I could hear the music grow louder and louder. It was so beautiful. Like a thousand symphonies playing as one, yet each in accord with the other. The child/angel let go of my hand and bade me to step towards the direction from which the music was coming.

'Follow,' he/she said, 'they are waiting for you.'

I did so without hesitation.

CHAPTER 24

Michael, Age 19
Queensland, Australia, 1999

The next few days were as close to heavenly bliss as I could remember. Angela and I explored both the simplicity and depths of our love for each other. Gone was any sense of puppy-love infatuation or teenage misconception of love and all its facets. This thing was real. It was tangible.

We spent time ambling along streets without anywhere else to be. We sat on riverbanks that told us we were in love. We ate in sidewalk cafés that had no one else in them except us two. We made love on the golden sand of the nearby beach under the watchful eye of a full moon. Even meeting her parents for the first time was relatively benign. I guess it must have been the way we looked at one another that told them both how serious our relationship was.

Angela knew I had to return to my duties in a few days' time, but that only heightened the anticipation of our next touch. Fingers seeking fingers, a soft caress to a sleeveless arm, the catch of a glance of eyes full of love. Everything had meaning and required no further explanation. We spoke of our dreams for the future and our plans for a well-founded life with money, happiness and health.

I didn't plan it. I didn't even think about a ring. But that night sitting in the restaurant overlooking the bay seemed like the perfect time. I asked Angela to marry me. My heart didn't even skip a beat when I asked, but the time between asking and her response felt like an eternity. It was her tears that broke the moment into pleasure. Tears of happiness for her, tears of relief for me! We even celebrated with a glass or two of an outrageously expensive bottle of wine. *Oh well*, I mused, *it's not as if I'm going to be doing this more than once in a lifetime.*

News of our intended nuptials drew much backslapping from her father and more tears of joy from her mother. The later evening was spent over far too many drinks with her dad, so much so that I only half remember that we were both talking in a language quite unintelligible to anyone else until the approaching dawn. The next morning, however, was a completely different story.

They say that 'no plan ever goes to plan' and that life requires a certain suppleness to weave through its' ever-present and often unforeseen pitfalls. With a head pounding like a thousand drums and a stomach not far removed from throwing up, the phone in the hallway rang and my future mother-in-law went to answer.

'It's your commanding officer at the base. I think it's something important,' she said when she returned to the kitchen.

I stumbled out to take the call, not really capable of thinking what it might be about. It must have been the look on my face when I returned to the kitchen that made everybody stop in mid-conversation.

'My leave has been cancelled,' I said feeling the bile from my stomach rise to my throat. 'I'm being shipped out to some war-zone in the Middle East. Effective immediately.'

The smash of the plate on the floor that Angela had dropped completely filled the void left by my words.

Angela's mum didn't help much because she started to cry. But her father was strident in his belief that 'we all have to do our duty' and that 'everything would be alright'. 'It's probably some minor skirmish between warring factions that will be over soon. You'll be back before you know it,' he said, trying to make everybody feel better. Angela was the only one who didn't say much, but I could see the tears behind her eyes that she was trying hard not to let out.

I never was one much for drawn-out goodbyes. I'd always preferred to just get on with it, not linger and not turn around. But this time was like having a root-canal without the gum-numbing injections. I tried my best to keep a lingering picture of Angela's beautiful face firmly in my mind. I even took a couple of mental snapshots and placed the images firmly in a welcoming door of a special room in my mind. It was the best I could do under the circumstances.

I had to go. The taxi was waiting. Angela touched my cheek gently as we said a lasting goodbye, then she removed something from her dress, kissed it gently then told me to bend my head down a little.

'Wear this,' she said firmly, 'it will protect you. It has magical powers of love.'

I took the heart-shaped locket between my fingers and placed it gently to my lips, but the taxi's toot was enough to shatter the moment. I turned without a further word and strode with leaden boots to the awaiting transport – the beginning of a journey to a foreign land with only the binds of love to provide comfort. I couldn't help but look back over my shoulder as I opened the door and entered the taxi.

The bus was nearly full but I still managed to find a seat to myself so I didn't have to talk to anyone. It didn't make the miles go any faster but at least I was able to let my mind drift over the memories of my time with my future bride. The problem was, the memories began to fade the further I was removed from the source. They were replaced with the endless possibilities of my pending deployment. I wondered, absently, if anyone had heard of this little-known war-zone, let alone cared. I did my best to distract my thoughts with taking aim at imaginary targets. Relax, ease my muscles into the soft earth, feel the strength and direction of the breeze, focus the mind, adjust the aperture, move a steady hand to the trigger, feel the cool metal on my fingertip, squeeze gently ... fire! I was so engrossed within the labyrinths of my mind I didn't even notice that the bus had stopped and new passengers had embarked.

The old man looked as if he had endured a life of trials. His face was a roadmap of creases and crevices each with its own story written on them. He looked at me with a nod as he placed his worn rucksack under the seat and sat down beside me. He didn't offer to speak, only nodded again as he adjusted his aged body into his seat's dubious comfort. As the bus pulled away, the old man just stared straight ahead and didn't flinch a muscle for many miles. I tried a couple of times to think of something to say but it all became too hard. I settled back and closed my eyes.

I'm not sure what it was that caused his sudden movement, but all of sudden he reached down into the backpack at his feet and removed a small black box. His movement caused me to open my eyes, and I watched as he lifted the lid on the box. The box contained a medal – a service medal. On first glance, it looked vaguely familiar. It was gold-plated with a Federation star surrounded by a circle of flames. I recognised it to be the Medal for Gallantry in Action.

'Excuse me, sir; I don't mean to rude,' I interrupted, 'but is that the Medal for Gallantry?'

The old man looked at me with rheumy eyes. He wouldn't have realised that I was in the service because I was dressed only in jeans and a tee-shirt. Anyway, at least it got the conversation started, and I told him I was about to be deployed to a conflict in the Middle East. He told me a little about his time in uniform. It was interesting hearing from the veteran, although

I sensed that he was only skimming the surface of his memory banks when recollecting his service to his nation.

The bus continued to speed along the highway until our conversation started to run dry. That was until a question kept banging itself around behind my forehead, but I was hesitant to ask. Eventually, however, I couldn't help it.

'Sir, the medal,' I asked, 'what did it cost?'

The old man looked at me sternly as if deciding whether I was deserving of an answer to such a forthright, multi-dimensional question. I could see the wheels turning behind the roadmap of creases on his brow. It took more than a few full moments before he decided to respond.

'Son,' he replied, 'I've paid a heavy price in my life for this medal and my service to this country. Not to mention my family and all the people I love.' He paused and sighed as if he was trying to find more words that paid justice to the depths of his innermost feelings. 'But it's not this life that I'm worried about – it's almost done. It's the next that bothers me. Eternity is a long time, son.'

I stared at him open mouthed for longer than I should have, and it wasn't until the bus pulled into the next stop that I was able to shake the depths of the old man's concerns from my mind.

He didn't say anything more, just nodded as he picked up his battered old body and backpack and walked stiffly down the aisle and off the bus.

Matthew J. Cooper
Heaven

When I returned to where I belonged, Margaret was there to greet me. I said a silent prayer into the ethers for the grace of her presence and returned her hug and smile with equal fervour.

'I've missed you,' I said as I watched the love dance around her eyes.

'But you've been busy, haven't you?' she replied with more than a hint of knowing.

'Yeah, I guess so ...' and I spent the next full moments telling her of my encounters, both with the beautiful lady and the child-like angel and others.

'You've come a long way,' she encouraged.

I didn't quite know whether that was a question or an exclamation so I figured it best to ask. 'What do you mean?'

'You've evolved,' she said with eyes that began to glow with an inner light from somewhere else. Although the crease on my forehead must have told her that I didn't really follow. 'This process ... what you've been going through ... it's called evolution. That's what this is all about.'

'But ...' I said struggling for words that confirmed any sense of my simple understanding. 'I thought, I mean, if, if this is heaven, then aren't we supposed to be judged, or something? Like, things weighed in balance to find out if we can enter the pearly gates.'

'My love,' she said as she took my hands and placed them to her heart. 'It is difficult to understand, but this is not a journey of reward or punishment. It never was a question of what was "right" or "wrong", "good" or "evil". God does not require anything from you. Your experiences, the consequences of your actions serve only to help you realise who you really are.'

I took hold of her hands as I pondered the magnitude of her declaration. 'But ... all the people I killed ... all the suffering I caused ... surely I am to be condemned for my actions?'

'And have you not experienced the consequences of your actions since being here?'

'Well, I guess I have. I mean all of that pain, all of that suffering I caused others to feel ... I felt it all. It was terrible.'

'Yes, you have. And what do you know now?'

'Huh? I don't understand.'

'Look,' she said as she pointed towards the expansive scene unfolding before us. It was beautiful like no other I had ever witnessed. Amongst roaming hills of unimaginable colour and glory stood a host of angels, much like the child-angel I had been with before. And then I could hear it – the music. I could hear it clearly. More wonderful than anything I could ever imagine. It was a part of me as I was a part of it, no separation.

'They are waiting for you. They are waiting to take you,' she continued as I struggled to take in the beauty of my surrounds.

'They are? Take me where?' I exclaimed.

'Yes, they are. They are going to take you back ... back to where you belong. One with everything – no separation, back to the source,' she said with a beaming smile.

I looked longingly at the angelic host in the near distance and felt a tug on my chest when a thick silver cord illuminated like a thousand light bulbs. But Margaret held my hand steadfastly and turned to stand directly in front of me.

'But first there is something you must do. Something you have not yet realised. Somebody you have not yet faced.'

I looked at her curiously not really knowing what she meant, but I was happy to be led along the pathway. She turned and pointed towards a door, a dark, forbidding portal that had appeared out of nowhere.

'I can lead you towards the door, but only you can enter,' she continued.

I felt the cool, silken touch of her hand in mine as she led me towards the entrance. I felt the fierce heat emanating from behind the door with every step I took towards this doorway to hell. I looked at my wife with apprehension.

'Remember always that I love you. I always will. You are never alone.'

I felt her hand loosen from my own as I looked towards the door with a trepidation unlike I'd ever felt before. I took a long cool breath to ease my unease, then stepped forward and walked on, alone.

CHAPTER 25

Michael, Age 20
Middle East, 2000

I'd almost forgotten that it was my birthday as I stepped off the back of the Hercules aircraft with the rest of my company. But it didn't matter much right at the minute. I could never have imagined that the world could be so hot. Straight away the sweat clung to my back like a wet magnet. It clawed at my throat and mixed with the sand and dust blowing across the tarmac from the vast desert I'd seen from the sky.

I watched this new world pass by through the dusty window of the heavily escorted bus that was taking us to our garrison post. For me, not ever having been outside Australia, this was akin to an alien landscape. I could draw similarities to the roughness of the outback of my upbringing, but this place looked like a moonscape. The abrupt change in environment, smells and cultural dislocation was hard to get my head around. One of my buddies on the bus yelled, 'Look out, the infidels have arrived' out the window as we were passing a local bazaar. It gave me the creeps, a bit. But I suppose to the Bedouin owners of the land, that's what we were – invaders, infidels.

We'd been here only a few weeks and as yet had not been summoned to action under fire. But we sure as hell trained. We trained until all we could do was to collapse exhausted onto our respective bunks each night. This night was no different. My bones ached with fatigue and my body, despite its youth, felt as if it were due a complete recondition. Despite this fatigue, I still felt it. I knew what it was because I had sensed it before. It was an itch that had to be scratched, a strong compulsion to execute. I reached into my kit bag and retrieved Grandpa's old diary. It certainly wasn't standard issue equipment, but I didn't care. Where I went, it went.

I lay there on the harsh comfort of my bunk, closed my eyes and did my best to bring Grandpa's clearest image to my mind. It wasn't hard. He was in one of the front rooms of my mind. I held the diary in my hand and allowed the energy of times past to surge through my veins, just like I'd done before – then I opened the cover to the page of fate. It was a handwritten entry much like many of the others. I started to read:

Not sure how much more of this I can endure. I haven't slept in three nights. Even when I do I can't escape the images, the nightmares. I hear their voices. It's like they're waiting for me.

I killed two more of the enemy today. Shot them both through the heart - no suffering that way. I guess it doesn't matter anymore anyway. I've killed so many. Problem is, I'm starting to feel angry at everything. I don't know why. It's just that everything anyone now does really pisses me off. An infantryman made some aside comment about snipers in the pub the other night. I nearly ripped his head off. Lucky someone was there to stay my hand otherwise I really would be in trouble with the MPs.

I wonder where all this anger is coming from? I mean, it's not as if I have some anger management issues or anything. I just don't get it. I guess the sooner I get out of here the better. At least then I'll be able to get back to a life without blood, death and horror.

It's funny, you know, when I try to sleep I hear all of these voices, but through all of the voices I hear, I hear crying. It sounds like a child crying. I can feel their tears hot against my cheeks. My chest pounds with their suffering. I can't breathe. I hope I haven't killed a child! I don't think so. What then?

Not very funny any of this stuff, is it? I suppose that's just the way it is, though. I'll get through it! Maybe I better start praying.

Bugger me, I thought as I closed the cover and replaced the diary within the security of its confine in my sack. *Poor Grandpa really was doing it tough. He never said. I never knew. I guess I was too young to know ... I hope none of that stuff happens to me.*

I confess that I had trouble sleeping that night. I kept hearing a child crying in my dreams and I felt a terrible fire emanating from one of the rooms in my mind. It kept me up all night tossing and turning in the heat. But the booming voice of our CO at 0500 hours was incentive enough to get moving. We all bustled to get ready. We were going on our first mission.

Matthew J. Cooper
Heaven

Hesitation, procrastination and fear-based excuses I found aplenty, all in the space of a moment. I thought of every reason under the sun not to enter the portal. I felt a tightening in my chest, and a cold shiver flood through my being. Although I still don't know how everything worked in this place, experiences sure felt real. I turned to place a final glance at Margaret in the hope of redemption, but she had already disappeared – to where I did not know.

Despite the tightness in my chest, I took a long breath and placed one foot in front of the other, each of which required conscious thought. I watched as my hand reached for the door handle. It was hot – everything was hot! It felt as if the blast from a thousand infernos was breathing behind this doorway to the indescribable. The sound was the other thing. It made the contents of my stomach churn, and I almost made fast to turn around and run. The child's scream echoed like a hundred fingernails scratching down a blackboard. I watched as my hand trembled on the door handle. Despite my palpable trepidation, I turned the handle, ever so slowly. The force of the heat that hit me as I pushed the door slowly ajar felt like the power of a volcanic eruption. My eyes watered, and it was all I could do not to cover my ears from the screaming.

'What ... who are you?' I said as my voice cracked under the strain of fear. The only response I received was higher pitched screaming. My mind was racing at a million miles per moment as I could do nothing else but give voice to my own torment.

'In the name of God, stop it! Whoever you are, for the love of mercy, stop. I will help you if I can, but please stop screaming,' I pleaded. This seemed to have some effect at calming the afflicted, for the high-pitched wailing started to subside slightly and convert to heavy sobs filled with laboured gasps for breath.

I took another step forward and wiped my eyes with my sleeve to try and make sense of the scene before me. It was almost impossible to see. The firestorm wall in front of me was like an impassable barrier between myself and who/whatever lay behind the veil of flames. I didn't know what to do. I could not move forward and had only the door behind me. I reached for the only thing I thought might work, my avenue of last resort.

'Margaret, help me, please,' I said out loud into the ethers, 'I don't know what to do.'

You know, I've heard it said that love knows no bounds or barriers, and I guess it's true because I heard her words clearly, as if she were standing next to me.

'Reach out, you must reach through the flames. He cannot come to you. You must go to him.'

Although I heard the words they didn't make much sense. I mean, I knew if I even got close to the flames I would be burned to cinder.

'But, I can't. It will destroy me,' I replied into the ether.

'Trust. Do not fear. Trust.'

I guess when you were at your most fearful, that's when you were most vulnerable to either good or bad advice. This time was no exception, and I figured that Margaret's love was about the best advice I was ever going to get. I knew she would never lead me astray, and even if it did, it was worth the price of love. I took another step forward in deference to the heat and reached out my hand. I watched as my hand lifted slowly and moved towards the wall of heat and flames. I saw my hand trembling as it inched towards its objective. I could feel the heat singeing the skin of my fingers. Then I touched the wall of flame. Oh, my God! It was cool! I watched as my hand pushed through the wall of cold flame. It wasn't real. I took another step forward and watched as my arm disappeared through the wall. No pain, no singed flesh, only blessed relief. The rest of me followed my arm. I walked through the wall, but what waited for me on the other side was something I could never have imagined. Not in a million years.

The child who sat before me had ceased screaming, but I could see that traces of tears had run rivulets down his reddened cheeks. His meagre clothing was tattered and filthy as if they had not been washed for decades. The boy-child who stared at me with eyes that pierced my soul could not have been more than eight or nine years old. I could only stare at the desolation on his face, but did my best to find my voice.

'Who, who are you?' I managed to stammer.

At this, the boy could only reply with another piercing scream.

'Stop, please stop,' I pleaded as my hands went involuntarily to cover my ears. 'I cannot help you if you do not stop screaming.'

Thankfully, he did, although my mind was a jumble of words that could not find a voice to make any difference.

'Don't you know who I am?' asked the boy. Mind you, these words came out of the child but they were in an adult's baritone voice. My forehead creased both in fear and complexity. *I know that voice*, I thought. *Where has it come from? Who is it? Who are you?*

'I'm sorry, I do not know you, do I? Should I?'

The child lifted his head and from his small throat came a scream more piercing than those that had preceded it. Again, I pleaded for it to stop.

'You come here to help, but you cannot. Leave! Leave me be. You are useless! You should be ashamed!'

I confess that these words did strike a chord.

'Who the hell are you to tell me I'm useless? Who do you think you are? You don't know me. You don't know what I've been through to get here.'

'You did nothing back then, so what difference will it make now. It's too late. It's all too late,' the boy-child replied stridently.

I stared at the boy as his words echoed through my shattered being.

'What do you mean, "I did nothing then?" What the hell are you talking about?'

The boy could only close his eyes. It was as if he were trying to find some inner resource to prolong his interaction with me. Moments passed into minutes before he raised his hand and pointed. As he pointed, an image formed like the scene on a cinema screen. I could only stare open-mouthed at the kaleidoscopic visions that unfolded before my eyes …

I could only see his back, but he was a brute of a man. Six foot three and two hundred-plus pounds. I could feel his rage. Heat emanated from him like an out-of-control bushfire. The belt in his hand flayed repeatedly like a whip across the back and legs of the poor tormented woman under his wrath. I could see the red welts appear on the bare-back and legs of the unfortunate female he was beating unmercifully. The only thing I could discern between flaying lashes were the stifled cries of anguish and pain as flesh was rendered from her body. The strangled, tortured cries from the poor helpless woman under sufferance of the brute's beating. ...

I felt something akin to bile reach for my throat. My hands clenched in repressed anger at the scene unfolding before me.

'Stop it, please. I've seen enough. Why are you showing me this?' But he did not listen. I could barely turn my sight from the screen to see the child weeping softly as his little chest heaved great sighs trying to right itself.

Then, as I turned again to the unfolding nightmare on the screen, I heard the whimpering. I saw the child. It was the same child now seated before me. He was cowed behind a dilapidated old sofa a mere few steps from the scene of continued beating. I watched as the child bit into his hand every time the belt struck – as if he were himself being flayed. His face was a tangled mass of wretched anguish as tears poured down his dirt-encrusted cheeks to fall on the worn carpet on which he trembled in fear. The little boy rushed to his distraught and damaged mother when the beatings finally ceased and the brute left the room, chest heaving as he replaced the belt through the loops in his pants.

'Mum, Mum, I'm sorry, I'm sorry. I didn't know what to do. I'm useless. I'm so ashamed.'

Then, mercifully, the cinemascope stopped. It was all I could do to stay upright as I felt my legs buckle and threaten to collapse from under me.

'Now do you see?' said the child as he stared at me with eyes burning with fire.

'Oh my God,' I replied. My lower lip trembling as I spoke. 'But, it wasn't your fault. You were only a child. How could you have done anything to stop it?'

'You still don't get it, do you?' said the boy with a sneer as he stood up and walked the few paces to stand before me.

Then it hit me like a bullet. The force was like a thousand punches to my solar plexus. I felt a sharp pain in my stomach as my hands went to cover my mouth. I now understood. I understood everything.

'It's, I, you ... You are me! ... That boy ... that's me, isn't it?'

The child merely blinked his response. It was enough. I collapsed to my knees and held my hands to my face as a hot wave of tears fell like an avalanche down my face. The sobs racked my body with uncontrollable spasms. I cried, I screamed. 'No, no, I'm so sorry. I didn't mean to be a coward. I couldn't help her. I couldn't help any of it.'

'Yes, I know,' he replied softly, but it was his voice that made me startle. It was no longer the same voice as before ... my voice. That voice I now recognised. It was now a child's voice ... my childhood voice.

In the whole of my existence, I had never felt so tired. It was as if all of the energy of my being had been sucked into a swamp of pain. I could do nothing but look up from my knees at the child standing before me.

'What do we do now?' I managed to croak as I watched his eyes reflect the depths of his own unknowing.

'I don't know,' he replied in equal angst.

The moments that passed between us felt like a millennium of lifetimes. There was no time, only a wasteland of a lifetime stretching before me. That was until I heard something. It was music at the edge of a distance, far away but not that far, only getting closer. I heard the words drift across the soft cadence of the melody.

'You must forgive. Forgive yourself. Only then will you be healed. Only then will you glory at your own highest self.'

We both heard the words. I know I did. I know he did because I saw it in his eyes. It was in that same instant we both knew what to do. We reached out one to the other and held each other in a grasp of enduring embrace. We didn't know what else to do. That's all we could do. There were so many repressed waves of anguish that passed between us. I felt his small chest heave with a thousand sobs. Tears fell between us to mingle and share upon our cheeks. They fell and they fell some more – then slowly they began to abate. What before was a cascade, now was but a mere trickle. They were a trickle until they stopped and when they stopped they were replaced – they were replaced by a chuckle. Wrapped in each other's arms, we felt it rise within our chests. Slowly at first, then with ever more power. The chuckle turned to laughter. We laughed and laughed until our stomachs hurt and salty water again coursed down our cheeks. But this was water of release, of happiness, not of pain.

It was enough. We were both spent. Happily spent. I watched as the child that I was smiled at me with eyes that now reflected innocence, not anguish – we had been forgiven – by ourselves. I watched as he held out his hands to me, and I took them in my own. I heard as he said that he could go now. He was okay, and I was okay. It was time to go. I smiled my understanding as I let go of his small hands and watched as he faded upwards into the ether above me.

I turned slowly to see that the wall of fire and heat was no more. The pathway to the exit portal was clear. I walked towards the door.

CHAPTER 26

Michael, Age 20
Middle East, 2000

This was urban warfare at its most acute. I had found an elevated position on a dilapidated rooftop behind and adjacent through the cramped alleyways of the city's confined Medina – the city within a city. I had as clear view both forward and across as much passageway I was ever going to get in this restricted urban jungle. The Company's orders were simple. We were to clear the area of enemy combatants, the militants, the terrorists ... whoever they were.

How am I supposed to tell who is the enemy and who are civilians? I wondered. Are they terrorists or freedom fighters? They all looked the same to me. The long flowing robes, the turbans and veils. I suppose it all came down to if they were holding a gun and where they were pointing it. I reckon it must have been easier in Grandpa's day. At least the enemy wore different uniforms so you could tell which side they were on.

I fixed my tripod to the concrete floor and took aim through the windowless aperture of the derelict rooftop and eased my body into a prone position with as much comfort as I could manage. An abandoned mattress from one of the deserted rooms provided a modicum of relief.

My job was really simple. I had to protect our lads. My platoon of buddies who were risking life and limb to sweep out and kill those who would do us harm. I adjusted the aperture of my scope and made a slow broad sweep of surrounding windows, portals and any other cranny or crevice that might contain an enemy combatant.

'All clear, here, sir,' I said into the small microphone attached to the lapel of my flak jacket.

'Affirmative. Keep a keen eye out. The militant bastards are there all right,' came the response from my CO safely ensconced in his office back at base.

I heard our lads approaching long before I saw them. It wasn't hard, the roar of the Humvees and the grind of gears through the narrow confines told me all I needed to know. I watched as the pride of men exited in well-drilled formations from the rear of the vehicles. They formed scampered lines for cover under nearby awnings and barricades. It was then I caught a glimpse of sunlight reflection on metal. The barrel of the rifle appeared through an adjacent upstairs window moments before I saw the peering head of its bearer. The turban and gun-barrel told me all I needed to know. I fixed the range at one hundred metres, an easy distance for my skills. The wind wasn't a factor within the close-knitted confines of these streets. If it hadn't been for the odd vision of a sun still menacing the world outside the city walls, we'd wonder if there were even a sun at all.

Everything came down to this singular moment in time. Thousands of hours of practise and so many cardboard targets hit near enough to bulls-eye. Decisions had to made. In my hands, I held an instrument of death – but without me it was nothing but a complex design of metal and wood. I was the one in charge – a master mariner holding the tiller.

I took a calming breath and felt the air's cooling graces flow through my body like an elixir. My index finger moved gently forward until it felt the cool metal of the trigger. I fixed the enemy in my crosshairs. No hesitation – it wasn't time for conscious thought – I fired. I felt the sharp familiar recoil to my shoulder blade as I watched the man's head explode in a splash of blood and bone.

'Target down, sir,' I said softly into the microphone.

I heard the CO's response through my earpieces.

'Good shooting, Private.'

'Yes, sir,' I responded quietly.

But I didn't have time to wallow in the success of my first kill. All hell was about to break loose. The cacophony of elevated voices and gunshots in my earpiece told me all I needed to know. There was more work to be done.

I killed three more terrorists by the end of the day. All it took was one bullet each. I didn't miss. I aimed to kill and that's what I did. They were the enemy, but I didn't want them to suffer. That wouldn't have been right. Kill or be killed. Kill them before they killed me, or my buddies. That's just the way it was.

We all returned to base safely. I, for one, was grateful for that. But what I didn't know was that I was to be the 'cause-celebre' of the evening. I was summarily backslapped and showered with a good-natured bravado. Maybe it was just a cover for blessed relief by the members of my company who had returned without loss or injury, but I didn't mind. I must confess that despite not seeking any such acclaim, the positive reinforcement of my actions under duress was not without its effect to my ego. Normally, I would refrain from participating in any of the testosterone-filled banter and mayhem of the mess area, but this time I consented to the overwhelming peer pressure. Beers and banter flowed freely.

But we've all been there. There comes a point in alcohol-fuelled frivolity when we either stay or we go. If we stay, it means an ever-quick descent into the effects and consequences of the excess. If we go, it means we are able to wake up the next morning feeling as if we are still a wholesome part of the human condition. I deferred to the latter, but the decision did have its consequences.

I managed to slip out of the mess tent without too much ribbing from my inebriated comrades-in-arms. Anyway, I reasoned, if they wanted me to shoot straight the next day, they better well leave me to rest in peace.

On my way back to my tent I stopped by the latrine to relieve myself of the significant number of beers I had consumed.

I heard the stifled cough over the sound of my relief into the metal trough. After exhaling my relief and zipping up my fly, I went to investigate.

I'd seen him before, of course. He was a part of my Company. I knew him as a quiet lad, who couldn't have been more than nineteen years old. He was sitting in the shadow of the latrine with his back against the wall. I could see his hand tremble slightly as he removed the lighted cigarette from his mouth.

This wasn't my job, I thought instantly. *I'm no counsellor! That's someone else's department!* Despite these errant thoughts, I sat next to the young infantryman and asked for a cigarette that I didn't smoke.

I knew for certain what he was feeling. I'd felt the same on the edge of my reason before we were shipped into action this morning. He was scared. Now that was perfectly understandable under these conditions of human extremes.

'What are you going to do?' I asked, watching his face as he took a deep drag on his cigarette.

He looked at me as if I were from another planet. Being where we were, this was not too far removed from sensible reality.

'Whaddya mean?' he said with a country drawl that felt almost familiar.

'I dunno,' I replied seeking the same familiar twang, 'it's just that we've only just begun. Do you know what I mean? Today was just the start.'

I watched as the tumble of thoughts behind his forehead bounced about with the on-going problem.

'Dunno,' he replied taking another drag of his cigarette. 'I suppose I'll get used to it.'

The hot night air crackled with my thoughts around his muted response. 'Hey, it's all right to be scared,' I replied. 'Man, if you aren't scared then I reckon you're about an inch away from a bullet yourself. And I reckon none of us is bullet-proof, are we?'

'Hey, man,' he said with raised ire, 'I ain't scared, all right!'

'Yeah, yeah, keep your shirt on. It's just that being scared is normal.'

We lapsed into silence for a few long moments.

'So what's the problem then?' I asked as I watched him light another cigarette with his trembling hand.

He looked at me sideways, deciding whether I was worth the effort of the gut-wrenching emotion it took to disclose his innermost feelings.

'It's the killin',' he said after having made the momentous decision. 'I was taught that killin' is a sin. My mum, God rest her soul, taught me that, 'what you sow you reap'. If you killed someone, you'd pay a high price and never make it to heaven. That's what she always said.'

I scratched absentmindedly at the sand between my feet as I pondered the depths of his dilemma.

'Yeah, I suppose your mum was right,' I replied. 'But that leaves you with a problem out here, doesn't it?'

'Huh?'

'Look. Out here, I figure we've only got one choice. It's either kill or be killed. It's them or us and f**k the consequences.

Know what I mean? Not much room for choice in any of that, the way I see it.'

He took another drag on his cigarette and nodded in deference to the soundness of my logic.

'Anyway,' I continued, 'I reckon it's not so much what we do; it's how we do it.'

He looked at me as if I was a creature from the black lagoon. 'What the f**k are you talking about?'

'Look,' I said, 'when I shoot, I aim to kill – no suffering. I do my job. I reckon that isn't so bad.'

He looked at me dubiously. 'Yeah, the bastards are filthy terrorist scum, anyway. It just seems right to terminate their evil arses, doesn't it?' he replied with a heightened sense of righteous conviction.

I'm not sure why, but what he said really riled me up.

'Look, man, I don't kill for revenge, or with a head full of hatred, or worse – just for the plain fun of it, do you understand? I just do my job, okay?'

'Yeah, sorry, man. I didn't mean to ...'

I managed to calm myself as I scratched forcefully at the sand between my feet. 'Yeah, no worries ... It's just that, at least then I reckon I won't have much to answer for when I meet the 'big fella in the sky'. Know what I mean?'

He looked at me strangely as he took another drag, but I noticed that his hand had stopped shaking.

'Yeah, I s'pose you're right,' he said with a wry smirk. 'Or as right as we're ever going to get in this crazy-f**ked up place.'

I watched as he stubbed out the remainder of his cigarette into the sand and got up and looked towards his tent.

'I guess I'll see you tomorrow on the arena of battle, then?' he said as he walked away.

'Yeah, I guess you will,' I replied as I rose to find my way to a dreamless sleep.

Matthew J. Cooper
Heaven

I walked back out of the portal to what only could be described as a cacophony. Not a cacophony of discord, mind. Rather, a symphony of harmony. I heard the music. It filled my senses with a lightness I'd never felt before. It was as if the music was me, and I was a part of the music. It felt like the very essence of my being was filled with an unchained melody. I could do nothing but open my arms wide in greeting to the majesty of it all. It was then the veils parted and I saw them ... all of them.

Beings of light, angels from heaven, avatars of majesty, they were all here ... for me. First among equals, at the front of the assembled, was Margaret. She stood regal and radiant with facets of light surrounding her like an aura of multi-coloured rainbows. Her smile was like the dawn of a new beginning. She walked, or more descriptively, floated towards me with arms opened wide.

'Now do you see?' she said as she cast her arms wide to envelop the host.

'Yes, yes,' I managed to stammer still in awe of my surrounds.

'All of that pain. All of those experiences of hurt and harm in your kaleidoscope. All that you have seen and done has brought you to this moment.'

'Yes, I understand,' I murmured as my forehead creased towards an errant question. 'But, what now? Is this it? Is this what it has all been for?'

'No, my beautiful man,' she said in that quaint voice that I remember so well. 'Now it is time for you to ascend.'

'Ascend? Ascend where?' I asked in serious ignorance.

I could hear the symphony of music growing louder and I could feel a magnetic tug to the centre of my chest as if it were drawing me to itself ... wherever that was. I looked down at my chest at the silver cord throbbing like a missed heartbeat. It was Michael's cord. I knew it. I looked up at Margaret whose face registered as much surprise as my own at the unforeseen intrusion to my ascension to somewhere.

'Margaret, it's Michael! Something is happening to Michael,' I said with undeniable urgency.

'Yes, yes, you must go, quickly. There is no time to lose.'

I nodded my agreement and plunged my hand into the hues of colour and light. In an instant, I was transported.

CHAPTER 27

Michael, Age 20
Middle East, 2000

'Far out!' I said out loud, 'this is shit-sandwich!'

The angles were all wrong. I could barely get a straight-line sight on any potential targets. The area was too confined, even from my elevated position. My scope was hardly any use through the tight-knit alleyways. I only had the narrowest field of activity through which I could even remotely try and protect my buddies. I could hear them approaching – ETA approximately two minutes. Not enough time to find another secure position. I called my dilemma through to the CO.

'Sir,' I said into my lapel microphone. 'This is a cluster–f**k! I can't see anything from this position. There's no way I can protect them. I have to embed myself.'

'Copy that,' came the reply as the Humvees came into view.

I quickly packed up my rifle and hastened down the decrepit stairwell, back out into the alleyway just at the same moment that my buddies poured out from the back of the Humvees.

My NCO, who had tuned into my radio communications, knew exactly what to do. He pointed two fingers towards his eyes, then pointed in the direction of the position at point he wanted me to assume.

*F**k, it's hot*, I thought as the sweat under my helmet dripped into my eyes. My nerves were linked to a fever pitch as I watched my buddies bustle through doorways and around corners not knowing whether a bullet to the head lay behind and beyond. I crept slowly forward. Each step an entry into a new dimension of the unknown. My finger twitched nervously on the trigger of my rifle. It was all I could do not to piss my pants as I felt my bladder try to relieve some of my tension. Then all hell broke loose. Bullets were pinging everywhere and the sound of shattered concrete and splintering wood filled the air like the barking hounds of hell. By reflex, I dived for the nearest cover. The block of ragged concrete wasn't much, but it would have to do.

The sound of multiple stressed voices in my earpiece told me that we were in deep trouble, but I couldn't see where the enemy fire was coming from. I was about fifty metres west from the rest of my company, but it may as well have been a mile for all the help I was. I scanned the area within my field of view and saw nothing, nothing but bullet-ridden buildings and battle-scarred alleyways. I began to feel a sharp pang of panic rise in my chest. Not because I was in danger, but because I was useless. I wasn't helping. My buddies were in trouble!

I could hear the gunfire echo through the narrow alleyways and the deafening silence from the fallen through my earpiece. They were dying, and I was bloody useless. It was then that I saw him appear around a corner. I knew who it was straight away. He was one of ours. But how did he become detached from the group? It was the young infantryman. The same young man I had spoken with the night before. I could see his face as plain as day. His eyes said it all. They were filled with a high-octane mix of terror and distress.

I watched transfixed as he inched forward gingerly with his back pressed firmly into the wall, his rifle pointing towards potential adversaries he couldn't see. Then I heard the shot. Blood spurted from the wound on his shoulder, and I could only watch as he collapsed in pain, dropping his rifle to the ground as he fell.

Everything happened by reflex when bad things like this happened. I mean, all of the training counted for nothing when you saw one of your own's life in peril. Everything started to happen in slow motion as I watched the shooter get up from behind the concrete pylon that had hidden his presence. I heard the echo as he cocked his revolver and pointed it towards his crippled adversary, walking with a smirk on his face towards my fallen comrade with the gun outstretched.

F**k me, I thought, as I looked through the cover of his turban to a face that barely held any life experience. *He couldn't be more than twelve or thirteen years old.*

I knew what I had to do. I knew what I had been trained to do. I was here to do my job and do it right. All I had to do was aim and shoot. Easy! I hardly had to aim, I was that close. That's what I did yesterday. That's what I was here for.

By rote, I prepared the gun for its purpose – breech loaded and cocked, safety off and ready to fire. I took aim as I felt my index finger twitch in anticipation of pending action. I took a quick glance away from the young militant and saw the peril of pending death spread over my comrade's face as he watched his enemy stride slowly towards him.

Why I just didn't shoot the little bastard then and there I will never know. It would have been so easy. But I didn't. I felt something strange. It was like something tugging on my chest. I looked down quickly but couldn't see anything. I could hear all of the yelling and errant orders blaring through my earpiece, but there was something else. Words, music ... something! It was like an echo from a distant land with a voice of recognition that escaped the knowing. But, in the heat of the overflowing moment, the words became clearer.

'There is a higher way. Trust me! Trust me!' I heard through the din of external clamour.

I guess I'll never know why I did it. Maybe it was just something I had to do in life. Follow my instincts, I mean.

'Put it down,' I yelled as I stepped out from the cover of my barricade. I wasn't sure if he could understand me. It didn't really matter because the pointy end of my rifle was focused at the boy's chest and spoke a language all its own. I saw the surprise mixed with fear in his eyes when he watched me walking towards him.

Then I heard it again, clear as a bell. 'Trust me! Trust me! There is a higher way.'

As I took slow deliberate steps towards my adversary, I lowered my rifle. I watched as he observed me disarm my weapon. I placed the gun gently on the ground. I saw the look of surprise register on his face that I was now disarmed and he wasn't. The boy was in control. He held the power of life and death in his hands. I watched as he cocked his gun in eager anticipation and turned the gun towards my chest. But his hand trembled slightly.

It was in that singular moment in time, some kind of inner-impulse took over. I held my free hand's palm out to him then slowly, very slowly, reached with my right hand towards the inside of my collar. He watched me with eyes that blared with confusion. I removed the heart-shaped locket from around my neck – the very same one that Angela had given me on our parting. I held the locket in my outstretched hand towards him. I could see the conflict in his eyes.

Mere moments passed like hours as the play of a lifetime crossed the face of my young adversary. I could see the tapes running behind his eyes telling him that we were infidels who needed to be destroyed. But I also saw a flicker of something else ... compassion. It was there all right! I watched the two wolves as they fought behind his eyes. The black one or the white one – it was only a question of which one he was going to feed. I stared as his face crumpled and tears forced their way into his eyes. I saw him gasp involuntarily as his breath stuck firmly in his chest and refused to budge.

The sound of the click of his gun echoed through me like a twig's snap breaking the silence. I watched as he disengaged the firing mechanism of his revolver. He lowered the gun. It was the exact same moment that we could both breathe again.

Still holding the locket before me, I took two paces forward and pressed it into his hand and nodded to say that it now belonged to him. He looked at the tiny shimmering object as the sun glinted off it, then he looked up into my eyes. They said thank you in a language I understood completely. It was enough. I watched as he turned abruptly and scampered into the bowels of the walled-city from which he had come. I guessed he was running home to his mother – but maybe not.

I sped across to my prone and near-unconscious comrade while barking urgent calls into my microphone for a medevac. I did my best to compress the wound to staunch the flow of blood.

'Hang in there, buddy. Stay with me,' I kept repeating as the precious moments ticked away too slowly.

I watched as his eyes fluttered valiantly to hold onto consciousness. There was nothing else I could do to help him ... except pray. Then there was a flicker of an echo, just at the edge of my hearing. I swear it's true ... I heard it.

'Michael, I am here ... I always will be.'

I turned abruptly at the sound of the medevac's arrival. When I strained again to hear Grandpa, the words were gone, but by then help had arrived.

EPILOGUE

Matthew J. Cooper
Heaven

'Can we go now?' I asked with a wry smile to the beautiful angel that was my Margaret, who was waiting for me upon my return.

She really didn't need to utter a word. She merely held out her hands for me to clasp gently in my own. We both heard the music. It surrounded us. It engulfed every fibre of our existence. I still wasn't quite sure where we were going, but I didn't particularly care. I knew this to be the beginning. The beginning of what I wasn't entirely sure, I just knew it was heaven, but then again, it was all heaven, wasn't it. Everything. All of it.

Our eyes met in an eternal pact of the deepest love, and the depth of our smiles knew no boundaries as I felt the music lift us upwards. I saw them, the angels. I heard their song. We soared as we rose, still wrapped in the love that we would eternally share. We started singing, too.

We were going home.

Michael, Age 21
Canberra, ACT, Australia, 2001

I stood firmly to attention, but couldn't help the faint hint of a smile as the Medal for Gallantry was pinned to my chest. I suppose, when all was said and done, I did manage to save that young infantryman's life. Even though the details of how it was achieved will remain forever locked safely away in my mind. *Geez*, I thought, *I wonder what ever happened to that young militant boy?*

I managed a glance across to Angela, who was standing proudly in the gallery watching her husband receive the honour of his grateful nation. She looked radiant, and the bulge of her beautiful floral dress outlining the second trimester of her pregnancy only made her look the more adorable.

It wasn't as if I tried too hard to focus on the future. The present supplied more than enough happiness to fill my boots for a lifetime. The music from the military brass band filled the air with a rhythm that lifted the soul as I watched my other comrades-in-arms receive their respective and well-earned recognition. Then something caught the edge of my vision.

There, over by the large oak tree, just to the side of the parade ground. I looked then looked again, thinking that it must have been a trick of the mid-morning sunlight. But then I knew it was not. He was there.

It was Grandpa. I was sure of it. He was looking absolutely radiant. It was as if he were made of pure light. His spirit glowed like an angelic being from the heavens.

He smiled at me, and it was as if a thousand light bulbs all flashed at once. I saw him wave and I couldn't help it ... I waved back. I caught a glimpse of Angela looking at me strangely, wondering who I was waving at.

The day had come and gone and I was tired. After all of that pomp and ceremony, I just wanted to be alone with my wife. I reached for her hand that she took with a smile. Our eyes said all they needed to say.

'Let's go home, my love.'

Author's Note

Normally, before I start writing a book, I commence with something like a mind-map. That is to say, an outline of the ideas, topics, structure and storyline that provides a roadmap for the words and story to flow. Generally, this is enough to provide me with all the information I need to write the words as they have been laid out before me ... but not in this case.

The book *Bodies of Consequence* did not evolve in such a manner. It first started as a short story. I was content to leave the story as such until the portents of inspiration told me that there was more work to be done ... much more.

I confess, having such inspiration to write further did prompt me to try, in my usual manner, to 'mind-map' and outline the details of the novel. But it didn't work. Nothing happened. The tank was empty. The well was dry. It had never happened like that before. I could see neither structure nor story. When considering the storyline, I came up with a blank.

The gestation of this book was to happen in a completely different manner. It was given to me piece by piece – like putting a jigsaw puzzle together one piece at a time. I had neither concept of the ideas nor storyline that would form the basis of the narrative as I sat to write each of the ensuing chapters. In other words – I had no idea what I was going to write, nor what was to be related by way of the on-going story. It just came to me, without exception, every time I sat to write – one piece at a time. If I tried to see any further than that, it wouldn't let me.

For me, that means that the words and the story are divinely inspired. They have come from a source of 'knowing' beyond the rational comprehension of the logical mind. Hey, what do I know about life-after-death? I'm still alive and, if I did have any past lives, then I certainly don't remember much. I can only know what I have been told, or read in books, both sacred and non-sacred. That is not enough. That is not how this works.

The words and stories in this book are from a source I can only assume is working in our favour – to help us in some way or other. To prepare us for the consequences of the actions we take in this life we have chosen. I know this to be so.

If you seek to change your life for the better, for yourself and others, as a consequence of reading this book – so much the better for all who cross your path – both in the here-now and the hereafter.

Having said all that, it does take a great editor to make a book even better. My thanks to Juliette Lachemeier at The Erudite Pen for making it so.

Stephen Chong M.Ed. is a highly sought-after personal development coach, speaker and author. Stephen's many books have provided guidance and motivation to countless readers through his inspirational messages and ability to bring the best out in people. Stephen is a gifted 'storyteller', and his wise observations of modern life provide much insight on how to realise our highest potential through a rich and fulfilling life.

Stephen's unique talents as a storyteller are exemplified within his first four novels as he enables readers to 'find their inner hero' through the gift of story. Stephen's books include: *The*

Book of Testaments: A practical guide for spiritual realisation (2009), *The Music of the Soul: A pathway to a rich and fulfilling life* (2011), *Letters Across Time: A journey of enlightenment* (2013) and his fourth book, *The Power and the Possible: A teenager's traverse of the world* (2015).

Enjoyed the book? You can follow the author and leave a review at:

Stephen's blog site http://www.stephenchong.com.au

Web: www.stephenchong.com.au

Email: stephen@stephenchong.com.au

Facebook: www.facebook.com/stephen.chong.7906

LinkedIn: https://au.linkedin.com/in/stephen-chong-m-ed-38955046

CPSIA information can be obtained
at www.ICGtesting.com
Printed in the USA
LVHW101501290622
722393LV00004B/43